HARD WIRED

J. B. TURNER
HARD WIRED

THOMAS & MERCER

Text copyright © 2016 J. B. Turner
All rights reserved.

Published by Thomas & Mercer, Seattle

www.apub.com

Amazon, the Amazon logo, and Thomas & Mercer are trademarks of Amazon.com, Inc., or its affiliates.

ISBN-13: 9781503938328
ISBN-10: 1503938328

Cover design by Stuart Bache

Printed in the United States of America

For my two sons

One

The call came as night fell.

Jon Reznick was standing on the Rockland breakwater as the lighthouse beam swept over the dark waters of Penobscot Bay. The waves crashed off the granite slabs, sending cold spray into the air. He wondered who could be calling at this time of the evening. His cell number was known to only a handful of people.

When he finally answered, the voice on the line was a whisper. It had a sense of urgency about it.

"Who's this?" Reznick said.

Deep breathing down the line.

Reznick was about to end the call, but then the voice rasped angrily to life.

"It's Tiny, man . . . You getting this?"

Reznick's blood ran cold. He recognized the voice as that of an old Delta buddy, Charles "Tiny" Burns.

"I'm checking out, Jon."

Reznick could make out sirens in the background. "Checking out? What the hell's happened?"

"I'm trapped."

Reznick began to pace the breakwater. "Shit . . . Where?"

"Goddamn car . . . Miami."

"Christ."

"Bleedin' out everywhere, man."

Reznick closed his eyes. "I'll call nine one one."

"Paramedics are here."

"You're gonna hang in there, you understand?"

Tiny moaned and gasped as if trying to catch his breath.

Reznick pressed the cell tight to his ear. "Goddamn, Charles, do you hear me?"

"Jon . . . not gonna make it. I'm goin' down."

"Charles," Reznick said, raising his voice, "you're not checking out on me yet."

The sirens grew louder over Tiny's gasps. "Goin' cold. Real fucking cold, man."

"Charles, is there anyone in Miami I should call?"

"Too late, man . . ."

"What d'you mean?"

"She's gone. Wife and my boy aren't moving . . . Blood everywhere, man." He began to sob.

Reznick's mind flashed up terrible images.

"Cold. So goddamn cold, Jon. Can't feel anything, man."

"You will not fucking die on me, you hear? You will not fucking die on me!"

"Listen, Jon . . . you need to know."

"Don't talk."

"I have to, man. You need to know . . ."

Reznick closed his eyes. "Need to know what?"

A beat. "They got me."

"What?"

"Yeah . . . Be careful, man. They're gonna kill us all . . ."

The last moments of Charles Burns's life were played out in a mangled wreck on I-95, amid the skyscrapers and residential towers of downtown Miami. According to eyewitnesses, his car flipped over after he lost control. Paramedics arrived on the scene after two minutes, but there was nothing they could do. Major trauma to the heart, lungs, and liver, as well as a broken spine and two broken legs. His wife in the passenger seat and kid in the back were both killed as the car careened into oncoming traffic, as was the elderly driver of another vehicle.

Within the hour, the story had made the Metro section of the *Miami Herald* website, which described the crash in graphic detail. They quoted anonymous police sources, saying the driver might have fallen asleep at the wheel.

The following day, the *Herald* reported that officers close to the investigation cited the driver's "mental health issues," which may have contributed to the terrible crash.

The steady drip of stories continued for five consecutive days. And they covered everything there was to know about the former Ranger and Delta Force operator, who was dubbed "a good guy, but troubled" by unnamed former colleagues.

The newspapers and local cable channels built up a picture of a veteran who was having difficulties integrating back into society. They interviewed his neighbors in the low-rent Overtown area, just north of downtown Miami. And they pieced together, in gruesome detail, the final moments of Tiny's life.

They seemed to have the whole story. Everything, that is, apart from the call he made to Jon Reznick.

A week after the crash, under a perfect, blue Miami sky, Reznick stood on the periphery of the group of mourners at the Burns family's graveside, where the funeral of Tiny, his wife, Lanelle, and their eight-year-old son, John, was commencing. Tiny's family and friends held each other tight for comfort and support. Tears spilled down the mourners' faces as a few began to sob openly. It took six big guys to carry Tiny's coffin, while there was a smaller coffin for his wife, and a child-size coffin for his son.

The minister dabbed his brow with a white handkerchief and began to recite the Lord's Prayer as the coffins were lowered into the three plots. Then he read some passages from the Bible and talked of the man who had fought for his country. He didn't mention the time Tiny had spent living in a shitty trailer in Delray after a temporary split from his wife. And no one there heard about him working the doors of dangerous nightclubs and bars across Miami. The relentless grind of making ends meet.

As the harsh sun beat down on the mourners, Reznick's mind drifted. He replayed Tiny's final words over and over in his head. The sound of his voice. The desperation. But most of all, what had he meant by "*they're gonna kill us all*"? The words had been plaguing Reznick. He'd thought of little else in the days following the crash.

His gaze wandered around the seventy or eighty mourners. Standing on the far side of the cemetery was a fair-haired guy wearing a navy suit, white shirt, and black tie. Reznick recognized him as Pete Dorfman, a Delta operator from way back.

"Ashes to ashes, dust to dust," the minister said.

Reznick stepped forward and stared into the grave, as close family threw handfuls of earth onto the coffins.

After the minister brought the funeral service to an end, everyone hung around, exchanging commiserations and hugs. Then, as they drifted out of the cemetery, Reznick caught the eye of Dorfman, who smiled.

"Long time no see, Jon," he said.

Reznick shook his hand. "Yeah."

"Think everyone's heading down to the Deuce in South Beach for a drink. Where Tiny used to work. How does that sound?"

Reznick nodded. "Meet you there in an hour."

The Deuce was a windowless dive. Inside was a horseshoe-shaped bar with a pink neon sign flashing on and off. A Ramones song was playing full blast as Reznick and some of the others filed in. It was hardly a typical after-funeral venue.

A few disheveled barflies looked up from their drinks. Some family friends and relatives, along with members of Tiny's church, were looking a bit bewildered to be in such a place. Reznick was introduced to a few. He offered his condolences, and took a Scotch from Tiny's brother-in-law, an ex-Marine. He knocked it back, the warm liquid burning his insides. It felt good.

As he drifted away from the group, Reznick noticed Dorfman sitting by himself in a corner near the pool table. He went to the bar and ordered a couple of cold Heinekens, then walked over and joined him.

"Good to see you, man," Dorfman said, taking the beer gratefully.

Reznick sat down and looked at Dorfman, who had tears in his eyes. He clinked his bottle of Heineken against Dorfman's and took a long sip.

"You all right?"

Dorfman nodded. "Nothing some liquor won't cure."

Reznick smiled.

Dorfman nursed his bottle of beer for a few minutes before they began to talk. First small talk: the atrocious heatwave engulfing the South. Then they moved on to the old days, and the Delta crew they'd known and served with. But more than anything, they talked of Tiny.

"Goddamn, man," Dorfman said. "Why the hell didn't we keep in touch?"

Reznick took another gulp of beer. "Never seem to find the time."

Dorfman sighed, a faraway look in his eyes. "Must be a couple of years—maybe more, Jon."

Reznick finished his beer. "Yeah, must be. What you been doing?"

Dorfman leaned in. "Close protection, mostly. Consultancy."

Reznick nodded.

"VIPs, that kind of stuff. At the moment it's some rapper asshole. Even had to go on tour with the fucker for three straight months."

"Lucky you."

Dorfman gave a rueful smile. "Pays well, and we stayed in fancy hotels across Europe. But the guy . . . Major-league asshole." He shook his head. "Spend half my time sitting at the next table as this guy and his dopey hangers-on knock back bottles of Krug and Grey Goose, arms around some escort girls."

Reznick ordered two more Heinekens from a server, who was wearing a Velvet Underground T-shirt. "Couldn't imagine anything worse."

"Yeah, pretty much what I was thinking about seven every morning when I got to my bed."

"How did you hear about Tiny?"

"His cousin from New York called me."

Reznick didn't feel much like mentioning Tiny's last phone call. He looked over at the other mourners, who were mixing with the hipsters, boozehounds, tourists, and workmen filling up the bar. "Good turnout."

Dorfman glanced around. "Yeah—popular guy."

"Thought there might've been some more of the cadre."

"We all went our separate ways, Jon. People lose touch."

Reznick sipped his beer. "Yeah, I guess."

Dorfman clenched his fist. "Good guy. Real good guy."

Reznick drained the rest of his drink. "Damn straight."

Two

The sky had turned blood red by the time Reznick and Dorfman left the bar. They headed back to Reznick's nearby hotel—the Winter Haven—went up to the roof terrace, and kicked back with two more beers.

Reznick noticed a tremor in Dorfman's hand as he gripped the bottle. As the night wore on, Dorfman revealed he had served time in jail for a bar brawl. Reznick wasn't surprised. There was anger boiling under the surface. In fact Dorfman had been arrested numerous times for fighting in bars. Taking offence at imagined slights—someone looking at him the wrong way.

Reznick listened as Dorfman talked. His wife, Arlene, had left him because of his drinking, and he now lived with his eighty-year-old father in Fort Lauderdale. Dorfman got that distant look in his eyes again. He mentioned flashbacks of their Delta comrade Thomas Brading being mown down in Baghdad.

Reznick had seen countless guys going the same way. The descent into darkness, struggling to contain the demons that had been unleashed by warfare. Withdrawing into themselves. Shutting themselves away from the outside world. Closing themselves off from loved ones.

Dorfman gazed off across the art deco rooftops toward the ocean. "Bad thoughts, all the time. Trouble sleeping."

Reznick nodded.

"What can I say? Just the way it is. So, what about you?"

Reznick shrugged. "What about me?"

"What do you do?"

"Trust me, you don't want to know."

Dorfman took a long, hard look at him. "Man, you never change."

Darkness fell over the beach, and a gentle breeze blew in. Dorfman was getting drunk fast as the sound of bass-heavy music pumped out of cars headed along Ocean Drive.

Dorfman glanced at his watch and looked at Reznick. "I better be hauling my ass back to Fort fucking Lauderdale."

"Why not get a room here?"

Dorfman shook his head. "I'll grab a cab. Stuff to do tomorrow." He got unsteadily to his feet and hugged Reznick tight. "Good seeing you again, bro."

"And you, Pete."

"Keep in touch."

Reznick watched from the roof terrace as Dorfman hailed a passing cab and was gone.

Reznick snatched a few hours' sleep, and was up just after four. He showered, got dressed, and took a taxi to the airport. He sat in the departure lounge ahead of the early-morning flight to New York, gulping down his second black coffee of the day. His mouth felt dry after the booze, but he was neither up nor down after the drinks with Dorfman. He always knew when to call it a night—but it was clear his old friend had been hitting the liquor hard for years. The tremor in his hand, the way he finished his beers in three or four gulps. He'd seen it all before. Dorfman was an alcoholic.

His thoughts turned to the visit to New York. He knew his daughter was staying in the city as part of a trip around the museums and galleries in Manhattan. And he was looking forward to surprising her by turning up unannounced at the Guggenheim and taking her to dinner.

His cell phone rang and he checked the caller ID. It was Dorfman.

"Jon," Dorfman said. "Sorry to bother you so early."

"You OK?"

"No. I'm not OK."

"What's the problem?"

"Where are you?"

"Airport. Why?"

"You need to get a copy of the *Herald*, Jon."

"Why?"

"Just do it. I'll call you back in five minutes."

The line went dead, and Reznick wondered what had gotten into him. He sounded even more agitated than he had the previous night.

Reznick walked across to a News Express and bought a copy of that day's *Miami Herald*. He stared at the front page. Staring back at him was a huge photo of Tiny, alongside his dead wife and child, with the headline *MIAMI DEATH CRASH DRIVER DRUNK AT WHEEL*.

It took a few moments to sink in. Then he began to feel angry. It came from deep within him. Raw anger, until his head was swimming. He read the headline again.

"Fuck," he muttered to himself. Tiny was barely in his grave. And they were already accusing him, the day after he was buried alongside his wife and kid, of being responsible for killing them.

His cell rang and he headed out of the shop.

"Jon," Dorfman said, "you seen it?"

Reznick glanced again at the front page. "Yeah, I've seen it."

"Jon, this doesn't make any sense."

Reznick closed his eyes for a moment. "I know."

"What's going on, man? It's a flat-out lie. No way. No fucking way."

Reznick said nothing.

"The last time we met up, he's on club soda or Diet Coke or some shit. The guy did not drink. So what the hell are they writing a story like that for?"

Reznick knew that was correct. He tried to block out the loud-speaker announcement about his flight boarding.

"I mean . . . what the fuck, Jon? How can they write that?"

Reznick speed-read the story for a third time. "Look, I need to catch a flight."

Dorfman sighed.

Reznick felt as though his insides had been ripped out. And he knew Dorfman felt the same. He sensed his old friend's pain.

"Tiny was a straight-edge kind of guy."

The second loudspeaker announcement.

"They're not getting away with this."

Reznick was silent.

"Jon, we need to sort this out."

"I agree."

Reznick focused again on the facts. He knew that Tiny had been teetotal. His father had been a drinker, and that's why he never touched the stuff. He thought of all the times Tiny had stood by his side during firefights. Hunkered down in back alleys.

It was then that an idea began to form.

"Tiny never left anyone behind. He was one of us to the end."

"I know, Jon . . . I know." Dorfman sighed down the line. "So what do you suggest? What can we do apart from call up the cops and tell them they've got it wrong?"

Reznick looked again at the photo of Tiny. He remembered the look in his eyes when they'd escaped from Falluja in the dead of night. "We deal with this the way we always deal with things, Pete . . . right?"

"So how do we do that in this case, huh?"

"We keep it in-house. You know what I'm saying?"

"Jon, where you headed with this?"

"I want you to do me a favor, Pete."

"What's the favor?"

"You know any guys who could access certain information?"

"You looking for a computer guy?"

"Yeah, a guy that knows how to gain entry to systems and networks." Reznick closed his eyes for a moment as the plan began to formulate in his head. It was clear there had been a police investigation. He needed to find out what they knew. All of it.

"Sure, I know people that have that skill set . . . absolutely. But I've got to say—"

"Are you going to help me?"

"Help you do what?"

Reznick went quiet for a few moments as a noisy family rushed past. He waited until they were out of earshot. "I want someone to hack into the Miami-Dade Police computer system."

"Leave it with me."

Three

Reznick ignored the last call for the flight to New York. But the decision to change his plans at such short notice didn't sit well with him. He hadn't seen his daughter in months. His one consolation was that Lauren hadn't been expecting to see him.

He felt bad. But then he thought again of his old Delta buddy and his last words, and he knew in his heart of hearts that he needed to know more. He couldn't let it lie.

Twenty minutes later, Dorfman was back on the line.

"This is how it's gonna work. A friend of a friend is a private investigator. Fanatical about security. And this investigator, he vouches for this guy. Cyber-security expert, apparently. One of the best in America."

"I need to know more about him."

"This is what I know. This guy is ex-NSA."

"Ex? As in fired?"

"As in, *I can't stand working for peanuts anymore and I want to earn some real money.*"

"And he works out of Miami?"

Dorfman lowered his voice. "Here's the thing. This guy is using technology that's not even on the market. It's not even at the research and development stage. He's kinda out there, if you know what I mean."

"Is he good?"

"Good? Are you kidding me?"

"What I mean is, can he gain entry to highly encrypted computers without leaving a trace?"

"Jon, listen to me. This guy will get you anything you want. He's dropped out of sight of the government. Likes to stay on the move."

"So how do I call him?"

"You don't."

"What do you mean, I don't?"

"I mean you've got to speak to him in person."

Reznick didn't like the sound of the set-up. What kind of hacker wanted to meet in person?

"Why?"

"Why what?"

"Why do I have to speak to him in person?"

"He doesn't know you. And he'll want to know that you're serious about wanting this information and you're not some time-waster."

"So I don't have a choice?"

"He's holding all the cards, man."

"OK, set it up."

"Sit tight. I'll pass on your info to my intermediary, and then we'll see what happens."

⌣

He didn't show himself to the world. That came from his father, who hadn't been able to abide histrionics. Reznick's father had thought a person was unhinged if they panicked about being late or forgetting items from a shopping list. *No one died, so what's the problem?* His father had hated the latter part of his life, working that soul-destroying job in a fish-packing plant in Rockland. But he never bitched about it. He'd just put on that same impassive face and got on with it.

His father had seen death close up in Vietnam. Friends with limbs blown off, dying in agony, screaming for their wives or sisters or mothers. So why the hell would he bleat about how crappy his salary was, how shit his supervisor was? That was all bull.

Reznick could remember his father philosophizing with him, when he was growing up. *You suck it up*, his father had said, *and you move on. Deal with it. If you don't like it, shut the fuck up, or have the balls to leave your job.*

But his father hadn't been able to leave his job even though he'd wanted to. He'd needed to provide for Reznick. Needed to put food on the table. And he had. He'd brought up Reznick when his mother died, and Reznick had absorbed his mannerisms and matter-of-fact detachment from life. It had made him ideal for Delta. He could switch off his emotions almost at will and focus on the task at hand.

Reznick's thoughts switched back to the present situation. He knew Tiny was innocent. He was no drunk driver.

His father had always told him only to get involved in a fight you knew you could win. But in this case, he didn't know where the hell it would end up.

His thoughts darkened as he headed back into Miami and booked into a room at The Tides on Ocean Drive. He dropped his bag in the room and changed into a T-shirt, shorts, and his running shoes. He took a bottle of water from the minibar and set out on a morning run along the boardwalk, farther away from South Beach, past the hotels and towers fringing the beach that headed away from the heart of the Art Deco District. He passed other runners and walkers, many of them middle-aged fat guys, red in the face, bathed in sweat. He took a long drink of cool water.

Reznick felt the adrenaline surge through his body. He felt lighter. Sharper. Fitter. And happier.

On and on he ran as the sun burned his neck, listening to the sound of himself breathing in the sticky air.

Reznick returned to the hotel a couple of hours later, after doing some cool-down exercises on the beach. He retired to his room, showered, and put on fresh clothes.

He lay back on the bed and felt himself drift away. In his mind he could hear the sea and he was floating on cool blue waters. He was back in Maine, down in the cove, his daughter and his late wife splashing around beside him. He tried to freeze the image in his head. But almost as soon as it was formed, it dissolved into tiny fragments, blown away in the breeze, replaced by Tiny's voice, which echoed in the space. It seemed to bounce off the clouds. Reznick thought again of the hopelessness in Tiny's voice, as if he had accepted his fate. His words played over and over, reverberating in the darkest recesses of his mind.

He wondered what Tiny was getting at. Who was *gonna kill us all*? What made him say those particular words?

As Reznick mulled over these questions, he fell into a deep sleep.

The beeping of his cell phone snapped him out of his slumber. He opened his eyes. His room was dark. He checked his watch— 10:42 p.m. Then he leaned over and picked up his phone, and opened the new message. *People's Bar-B-Que, Overtown, Miami. Ask for Barbara. Be alone. Bring $1,000 in cash. And no phone.*

Reznick went through to the bathroom and splashed some cold water on his face. He took the SIM out of his cell and placed it with the phone in the hotel safe, alongside his gun. Then he went downstairs and hailed a yellow cab on Ocean Drive. The driver glanced in his rearview mirror. "Where to, bro?"

"Overtown. You know it?"

The guy winced. "Overtown? Are you sure?" He shook his head. "You ever been there?"

"No."

"Bro, you better be careful. Are you sure it's Overtown?"

"People's Bar-B-Que."

"Yeah, that's in Overtown. Area's a shithole, bro. Twenty-four-carat shithole. Garbage dump. You know that?"

"You wanna just drive?"

The driver nodded. "Not a problem, bro. A lot of the guys wouldn't take you there. But I ain't afraid."

Reznick said nothing.

"You going for food or something else?"

"Just drive and we're gonna get along just fine."

"Got to warn you, bro, those fucks don't value shit. Once dropped off a kid who wanted to score some dope. Read about him in the papers three days later. Shot in the head and dumped in an alley. Overtown, man."

The driver turned onto the MacArthur Causeway and drove fast across the bridge that linked South Beach with Miami. He didn't say a word after Reznick didn't engage him in further conversation.

Ten minutes later, the roads became more potholed; there were overgrown front yards, vacant lots, and darker streets. Broken streetlights. A few kids shuffling around on the sidewalks.

The driver pulled up outside People's Bar-B-Que. He glanced around at the surrounding streets. "You want me to hang around, bro?"

"I'll be fine. How much do I owe you?"

"Thirty."

The driver took the money Reznick handed him and shook his head. "Be careful, man."

Reznick stepped out of the cab and walked into the restaurant. The smell of spicy cooking and barbecued meats filled the smoky air. He sensed everyone in the restaurant was looking at him. He met each of their stares and everyone looked away, a few muttering under their breath.

A waitress came up to him. "Hey, honey, you wanna take a seat?"

"I'm looking for Barbara."

The girl smiled, brushing some hair from her face. "Not a problem, honey. Just go through the back."

Reznick headed through an alcove and into the back of the restaurant. A small twenty-something kid wearing a bandana was sitting on a ripped couch in the tiny staff room. "You Barbara?"

"Only on the weekends, man."

Reznick said nothing.

The kid cocked his head for them to go outside. Reznick followed him out a fire-escape door and into an alley.

"You're not far," the kid said. "Couple blocks from here, on the southwest corner of Northwest 8th Street and Northwest 6th Avenue, you'll find what looks like an abandoned warehouse."

"Who do I ask for?"

"That's all I know. Take care. And I mean *take care*, man."

The kid held out his hand and Reznick handed over a fifty-dollar bill. He winked and went back inside, leaving Reznick in the alley, trying to get his bearings.

He walked down the alley, crossed over the street, and headed away from the restaurant. He sensed he was being watched. Low-rise apartment blocks, an old woman staring down at him from her open window. He looked up, and the woman smiled down. "God be with you, son," she said as she shut her window.

Deeper into Overtown, past abandoned lots and boarded-up shops. A car slowed down and a guy shouted, "You want some coke, man?"

Reznick ignored him and kept on walking as the driver did a sharp turn in the street and blocked his path. The passenger jumped out and walked up to Reznick.

"I don't like people ignoring me, you understand?"

Reznick saw the driver grinning.

The guy pressed his face into Reznick's. His breath smelled of liquor. Reznick brushed past him and walked on.

"What the fuck you doing, man?" the guy shouted.

Reznick continued walking. Out of the corner of his eye, he saw a knife. He swiveled around, pushed the guy's knife arm away, and kicked him hard in the balls. The man fell face first onto the ground.

Reznick picked up the knife and threw it into a front yard. Then he kicked the guy hard in the head. He turned around just as the driver skidded away at high speed.

Reznick left the man lying unconscious on the ground and walked the remaining two blocks to the warehouse.

He turned onto a badly lit street, with broken glass and trash strewn on the sidewalk. Up ahead, in front of the warehouse, the lights from a car flashed three times. He walked toward the car. A young man stepped out with an airport-style wand scanner and ran it over Reznick's arms, legs, and torso.

"Clean," he said into a two-way radio.

The kid took a key out of his pocket and opened a box attached to the wall. He pressed his thumb against a fingerprint-identification scanner, and the outer door of the warehouse opened. "Come with me," he said.

Reznick followed him inside as the door slammed shut. Blue fluorescent lights came on automatically. They went into a cage elevator and up four flights to the top floor. The elevator stopped and the kid pulled back the metal door. He nodded for Reznick to leave the elevator and shut the door after him.

Reznick's gaze wandered around the space. As far as the eye could see was a loft-style apartment. Hardwood floors, white walls, air-con ducts, jumbo TV screens showing CNN and Fox News. But right at the far end, at a huge desk overlooking the Miami River through tinted glass windows, was a thirty-something guy wearing shorts, a white polo shirt, and sneakers. An Apple computer with a huge monitor sat on a pale-wood desk in front of him.

He turned and stared at Reznick.

"What is this place?" said Reznick.

"My office. Bought it for twenty thousand dollars at auction. One of the benefits of rampant foreclosures."

Reznick said nothing.

"You made it here in one piece. I'm impressed."

"So you're the guy I need to speak to?"

"Could be."

Reznick walked over to him. "I was told you could help me."

"Maybe I can. It all depends."

"On what?"

"I'm in the information business for a price. I provide information to individuals, companies, and voluntary groups—pro bono, so to speak—if I like what they're all about."

Reznick looked out the window.

"Nobody bothers me down here," the guy said. "Who the hell wants to hang out in Overtown?"

"You do."

"It's shit. Trust me, I grew up here. But the nice thing about it is, you're left alone."

"What about the cops or the FBI?"

"What about them?"

"Can't they trace your calls and stuff?"

The guy smiled. "What do you think?"

"What's your background?"

"MIT."

"And after that?"

"You ask a lot of questions."

"I like to know who I'm dealing with, that's all."

The guy nodded. "I worked for the NSA a while—you might've heard of them."

"So how come nobody's figured out you're working here?"

The guy rubbed his eyes. "I know how to mask what I'm doing. This warehouse doesn't appear on any Google map. It officially doesn't exist. Signal is jammed one hundred yards in all directions. Satellites can't pick it up. Encryption I use will be available to the military in five years' time, if they're lucky."

Reznick nodded.

The hacker pointed to a sofa adjacent to his desk. "Take a seat."

Reznick walked over and sat down.

"OK, I hear this is about a former Special Forces friend of yours. Sorry to hear about his accident. Read about it earlier. Said he was drunk as a skunk, right?"

"I don't believe a word of it. That's why I need your help."

The guy cleared his throat. "What kind of help? I need you to be more specific."

"I need original toxicology, traffic accident, and forensics reports on the death of Charles Burns."

"Interesting."

Reznick remembered reading a name in the *Herald* article. "Sergeant Francis O'Brien. He's the chief investigator for traffic accidents at Miami-Dade."

The hacker swiveled around in his seat and faced the huge screen. He tapped some keys, and within a few seconds, lines of indecipherable programming code were displayed. Ten minutes later, the Miami-Dade Police computer had been accessed.

"Voila."

He tapped a few more keys and scanned the names on the monitor.

"Got the toxicology report from the police lab."

Reznick got up from the sofa and stared at the screen. "Son of a bitch."

The hacker printed it out and handed it over to Reznick.

Reznick scanned it, double-quick time. "I don't understand. It says his alcohol count was three times the legal limit. That doesn't square with what I know about my friend."

"I'll see what else we can find."

A few minutes later, he said, "Something else concerning your former friend. Two items."

Reznick leaned forward and stared at the screen.

"Looks like the main report from the investigating officer," said the hacker. "And another from Rheinhart Traffic Forensics."

"You got that already?" said Reznick.

The hacker continued tapping keys, and the printer on his desk began to print O'Brien's report. Moments later, he handed over the nine-page document.

Reznick sat back down and read the report. It concluded that it was *reasonable to assume* that Charles Burns had been distracted or had in some way contributed to the traffic accident because of his intoxication, hence no skid marks.

Reznick felt sick. His buddy was getting blamed for his own death and that of his wife and kid. It stuck in his throat.

The hacker printed off the full forensics report on the car. It gave the Mercedes a clean bill of health.

Reznick shook his head. "Is that everything?"

The hacker gulped some coffee from a Dolphins mug. "One final thing. It's an addendum to the forensics report."

"But not in the forensics report?"

"Not as such. But it's here in the case files." The hacker printed off the addendum and Reznick looked through it. On the final page there was a picture of a circuit board, and a close-up of a one-and-a-half-inch part that drew his attention. The implications took a few moments to sink in.

"What is it?" asked the hacker.

Reznick read the passage in the report. "*The microchip transceiver (picture 1.1) within a circuit board of the electronic control unit (picture 1.2) was a non-Mercedes part and produced by Frieveson Electronics in Arlington, Virginia.*" He looked at the pictures again.

"What the frig does that mean?"

Reznick knew what it meant. Something was wrong.

The part may have been inserted to improve performance. But he knew there could be a more sinister explanation. He folded the printouts and put them in his jacket pocket.

"Is that what you're looking for, man?"

"Maybe. You want your money now?"

The hacker nodded, and Reznick handed over one thousand dollars in cash.

"Nice doing business with you, Jon."

"How did you know my name?"

The hacker grinned. "I make it my business to know things. By the way, you want any other favors, don't hesitate to contact me. Now I know you, you can reach me here." He handed over a card with a cell phone number. "Night or day. Take care."

With that, the hacker turned and faced the screen, and Reznick headed to the elevator.

Four

It was the dead of night when Mohsen Sazegara spotted Pete Dorfman getting into his car at the Four Seasons in Palm Beach. He was watching from the front passenger seat of an SUV in the same parking lot. The tracking device had already been fitted to Dorfman's car.

"Give him a minute's head start," he said to his brother, Behzad, before they pulled away.

A short while later, they were headed south on I-95. Mohsen checked the tracking device's location on his iPad. "He's half a mile ahead. Let's just keep it nice and easy."

Behzad nodded and reduced the speed to a steady sixty.

Mohsen checked the GPS of Dorfman's car again and pointed to the Fort Lauderdale ramp. "Nice and easy."

His cell rang. "Yeah, who's this?"

"Just a courtesy call to see if you guys are OK." It was their handler.

"Couldn't be better."

"He keeps irregular hours."

"We're fine. Don't worry about us. What about the footage from the graveside?"

"Very interesting," said the handler.

"How so?"

"It's taken some time to analyze all the footage. We're one hundred percent certain that the guy you're following is the right guy."

"Very much looking forward to acquainting ourselves with Mr. Dorfman."

"All in good time."

Behzad negotiated his way through the streets of an affluent Fort Lauderdale suburb. "Any intel on the target's house?"

"The father is in the house, along with a pit bull."

Mohsen felt himself wince. He hated dogs. Especially pit bulls. "We'll deal with the dog. How are you monitoring the father?"

"We've already activated his cell phone and are listening in. He's watching some game show crap."

"How very American."

"We did the same with the target's car."

Mohsen smiled. His handler had remotely activated the built-in emergency and tracking security in the target's car so they could listen in. "So, what's he saying?"

"He's been called by his old friend, a certain *Mr. R.*"

Mohsen knew the handler was talking about the number one target of the mission, Jon Reznick. "Do you think he was there yesterday?"

"We're still analyzing the cemetery footage, and there's one potential that fits the bill. He wore sunglasses and a dark suit, and he briefly chatted with Dorfman but we didn't pick up the conversation."

"Not to worry. We'll get to him."

"Like I said. All in good time."

Mohsen ended the call. The SUV hung back until the car was nearly out of sight. Then they followed as it negotiated the streets of downtown Fort Lauderdale, and on to a sketchy area on the periphery.

Up ahead, Dorfman's car pulled up outside a modest bungalow.

"Pull over," Mohsen said to Behzad.

The car came to a stop.

Mohsen picked up his binoculars and watched as Dorfman got out of his car.

"OK, tell me about this guy's habits."

Behzad turned to face Mohsen and said, "He's doing some security consultancy for a rapper named Getto. We're not going to get too many chances with him."

Mohsen watched as Dorfman went into his house. Lights turned on inside.

"OK, target is now inside." He turned and looked at his brother. "What about girlfriends? Boyfriends?"

Behzad smiled. "Lives with his father. Divorce has hit him hard financially."

Mohsen said nothing.

"Either way, the sooner he dies the better."

Five

After the trip to see the hacker, Reznick returned to his room at The Tides and slept for five hours. He awoke at 7:30 a.m. from a dream he couldn't remember. He took a few moments to get his bearings. It was a full twenty-four hours since he'd seen the terrible headlines in the *Miami Herald* at the airport. He showered, then had room service bring up breakfast. He began to ponder the two pieces of information the hacker had managed to glean about Tiny's death.

The toxicology report had showed his old Delta buddy was over the drunk driving limit. He still didn't believe that was possible. But the most troubling piece of information was the microchip transceiver that hadn't been fitted by Mercedes.

He wondered why the police hadn't included this in the final report, since the forensics company had taken the time to point it out. Instead, the chief investigator had focused on the blood alcohol count.

It was a red flag—at least for him. He was sure he knew what it meant.

Reznick lay back on the bed for a few moments, but his mind was racing. He looked at his watch. It was nearly eight o'clock.

"Goddamn."

He sighed and dialed the number. He wanted to let Dorfman know. It rang three times before transferring to voicemail.

"Hey, Pete," he said, "you wanna gimme a call? Speak later."

His thoughts turned to Tiny and their time in Falluja.

Chaotic. Manic. Heightened senses. Adrenaline. Then, suddenly, they were back home. Everyone getting hammered. Apart from Tiny. He didn't like the taste, he'd said—to much mockery.

Reznick had ended up in a fistfight with a fellow operator, Dan Murphy, who was making fun of Tiny for being sober. He remembered it as if it were yesterday.

Shaking his head, he got up and went into the bathroom to splash cold water on his face. Then he got a can of Coke from the minibar and gulped it down. He felt better.

He headed to a diner on 11th Street, diagonally opposite the Miami Beach PD. As he sat there, he wondered if he shouldn't have just headed up to New York. As if on cue, his cell phone vibrated. He checked the caller ID and saw it was his daughter.

"Hey, honey," Reznick said. "How are you?"

"Hi, Dad. Just thought I'd give you a call to see how you are."

"I'm fine. More importantly, how are you?"

"I miss you."

Reznick sighed. He felt bad for changing his plans. "I'll visit soon, I promise. How's school?"

She groaned. "Gimme a break, Dad. Calculus, geometry . . . What's that all about?"

"Who the hell knows? But I want you to work hard, got that?"

Reznick was grateful that his daughter, at an all-girl's boarding school in upstate New York, was getting the best education she could. He'd read her reports. She was a straight-A student for sure. And her teachers said she showed promise in science.

"Where are you?" she asked.

Reznick knew his phone had been encrypted so his location couldn't be known to anyone but him—and probably the NSA—but still . . . you could never be too careful.

"Never you mind. Listen, I've got to go. I'm gonna be out of range for a few days. But I'll be back in touch by the weekend."

"Promise?"

"Promise. Love you, honey. Gotta go."

Reznick finished his coffee and went back to his hotel room, where he waited for Dorfman to call back.

It was night, and Reznick was in his darkened hotel room. He looked down at the neon-lit strip of Ocean Drive. The noise of pimp-mobiles, tourists, clubbers, and the thumping bass of passing cars, all filtering up to his room. In the distance, the moon shimmered on the black Atlantic Ocean.

He opened a window and breathed in the warm night air. Heard the sound of breakers crashing over the beach. He thought again of Tiny's funeral. And he thought of Tiny being buried in the rock-hard soil of a Miami graveyard, beside his wife and child.

He began to pace the room.

Reznick wondered why Dorfman hadn't called. He called his old friend's number again. But there was no reply, just the voicemail. Reznick wondered if he should just call on him at his home in Fort Lauderdale instead.

He switched on the TV to CNN, which was showing a car bombing in Peshawar. He looked at the mangled wreck on the screen, thinking of Tiny's car crash.

At that moment, an idea began to form.

Reznick picked up his cell and pulled up the number for Miami-Dade Police Headquarters on the phone's browser.

"I'm looking for the address of the vehicle impoundment lot for traffic accidents in Miami-Dade, please. Got a parts delivery."

"Who's calling?" the woman working the switchboard asked.

"Broward Tow Trucks."

"Try tomorrow morning, that'll be your best option."

"No can do. Need to get it across to them right now."

A long sigh down the line. "OK. What have we here . . . you're looking for Northwest 7th Street, between Northwest 3rd Avenue and Northwest 3rd Court."

Reznick pulled up the Google map of the area and studied it, including the street view images. He wondered when he should make his move.

He found a late-night hardware store on Alton Road, where he bought wire cutters, binoculars, a screwdriver, a knife, and a backpack.

Just after 1:40 a.m., he caught a cab at 14th Street and headed across town, a plan now in place. He got the driver—who'd spent the ride speaking non-stop into his cell phone—to stop outside a Publix all-night supermarket and pharmacy in downtown Miami. He went into the store and bought a Dolphins baseball cap and latex gloves, and put them in his backpack. Then he got back in the cab and asked to be dropped off two blocks from the impoundment lot. He handed the driver a fifty, and told him to keep the change. The guy just shrugged, continuing on with his phone conversation as he drove away.

Reznick surveyed the scene. He saw a chain-link fence surrounding the back of the building, and some low-rise apartments in a sketchy area near a busy road. He put on the cap, pulled it down low, and put on his gloves. As he approached, he could see cameras overlooking a huge floodlit lot of damaged and burned-out cars.

Not seeing any foot patrols, he crept around the periphery for twenty yards. Then he saw it, at the far end of the lot—Tiny's mangled, fire-blackened wreck of a car. He recognized the license plate from a previous trip to Miami.

Reznick figured he was about fifty yards from the vehicle, and shrouded by foliage from palm trees. He kneeled down, unzipped the backpack, and pulled out the wire cutters. He cut a yard-long vertical line in the wire, and pulled open the chain-link fence to make a bigger hole. Satisfied he had enough space to squeeze through, he put the cutters back in his bag and pulled out the screwdriver.

He scanned the area. The cameras were stationary, and his current position was a blind spot. But he knew that by going through the fence and approaching the car, at least two of the cameras would spot him. Were they being monitored? If so, he would soon find out.

Reznick crouched down low, squeezed through the gap in the fence, and headed for the car. He forced open the front passenger door with the screwdriver, then switched on a penlight and pointed it around the interior. The smell of charred leather filled his nostrils.

He quietly shut the door and prized open the hood.

He shone the light on the engine. His gaze fixed on a plastic fuse box on the driver's side. He leaned across and pulled off the box's cover. Then he unplugged the ECU connectors, unscrewed the bracket, and removed the electronic control unit to reveal a complex circuit board.

He spotted the wireless transceiver, lodged into one of the ports. He got out his phone and photographed it from different angles, getting the consignment number—*THR4870303*—and serial number—*03938369504837498*. He peered close and saw the name *Frieveson Electronics*, as mentioned in the forensics report.

Reznick knew such a microchip device was designed to work in a modern car by processing information from the vehicle's sensors. It monitored everything from the outside air temperature to how much gas was left in the tank. Then it wirelessly sent all the data direct to the driver's dashboard. Why the hell would Tiny need to get a new one fitted? Was the old one broken? Or was there an altogether more sinister reason?

The smell of cigarette smoke in the night air snapped Reznick out of his thoughts. Moments later, he heard the sound of two men talking.

He let down the hood slowly and gently. Then he crouched down and held his breath. He weighed his options, and placed the penlight, cell phone, and screwdriver in his backpack. It was always better to get out while you can.

Reznick sucked some air into his lungs and padded across the lot. He squeezed through the gap in the chain-link fence, and disappeared into the night.

Six

The sun flooded through the wooden blinds of FBI Assistant Director Martha Meyerstein's office in the Hoover Building, as she studied a terrorism briefing paper ahead of a closed intelligence session on Capitol Hill. When her desk phone rang, she groaned and picked it up. She hated getting disturbed in the middle of work.

"Martha, you see what just dropped into our lap?" The voice on the line was that of her right-hand man, Special Agent Roy Stamper.

"This better be good, Roy, I'm up to my eyes in it."

"You should brace yourself."

"Why?"

"Reznick is back in business."

Meyerstein leaned back in her seat and sighed. "What?"

"A break-in at a Miami-Dade impoundment lot in the middle of the night. And they have footage of him."

"Are we sure about this?"

"The team working on face recognition pulled out his image. Because of his past connection to us, it sent out a red flag in our system. I've just emailed the file over."

Meyerstein pulled up the surveillance images on her laptop. Baseball cap pulled low, backpack on. It was Reznick. She could tell by the profile alone.

"How long ago was this?"

"Five hours."

"What do we know?"

"He left The Tides on Ocean Drive at one forty a.m. Then he caught a cab. Got photos of him buying wire cutters and a knife in a South Beach hardware store."

"Why's he in town?"

"Friend of his died. Delta operator."

"Name?"

"Charles Burns. Goes by the name Tiny."

Meyerstein closed her eyes for a moment. "Give me a rundown. Salient facts only, please."

"Charles Burns and his wife and son were killed. He was DUI. Car was impounded after the fatal accident. Now we have Reznick breaking in. That's the connection."

"But why?"

"I've read the forensic and police reports myself. Slam dunk."

"Where's Reznick now?"

"He's disappeared."

"What about cell phone tracking?"

"Nothing."

Meyerstein stared at the images. What was Reznick up to?

"There's more," Stamper said, interrupting her thoughts.

"Cut to the chase."

"This is where it gets interesting. Miami-Dade is saying, strictly to FBI computer techs, that there was also a successful penetration of their network systems in the previous forty-eight hours. But they can't trace where it originated from."

"Someone hacked the Miami-Dade Police Department?"

"Precisely."

"You saying the two things are linked?"

"This is Reznick we're talking about."

"What was accessed?"

"Forensic and investigator's reports into the death of Charles Burns, Reznick's buddy."

"What's Miami-Dade saying?"

"They're not happy. It makes them look like fools. And they know Reznick and the FBI are tight. They're going to think he's working for us."

"Use your contacts. Smooth things over, Roy."

"What about Reznick?"

"Find him. We need to know what this is all about. I can't have people breaking into police impoundment lots, no matter who they are."

"Miami cops think he's gone rogue."

Meyerstein stared out of her seventh-floor window and sighed. "Maybe he has."

Just then her cell phone rang. "Roy, I got someone else wanting to speak to me. Keep me in the loop."

She picked up her iPhone, not recognizing the caller ID. There was silence on the other end of the line, but she sensed someone was there.

"Who's this?" she said.

"We need to talk." It was Reznick.

Meyerstein got up from her seat, phone pressed tight to her ear. "Damn right we do. What the hell's going on?"

"You guys work fast."

"Knock it off, Jon. What are you playing at?"

"Friend of mine died."

"I know."

"They said he was drunk."

"And he was."

Reznick sighed. "That's a lie."

"Jon, you know how it works. The FBI can't be getting involved in your personal matters. You might not like the findings, but they are what they are. I'm sorry, it's just the way it is."

"That's bullshit."

"Listen to me. I appreciate you're feeling very sore and angry. That's natural. Your friend was drunk while in charge of his vehicle, and killed his wife and kid. But what I can't have is you actively engaged in illegal activities. Breaking into an impoundment lot, hacking computers—I mean, what are you thinking? I'm assuming you were responsible for that network breach?"

"You done?"

"Yes, I'm done."

"Two things. My friend didn't drink. A drop did not pass his lips as an adult. He hated the stuff."

"Stamper read over the police and forensic reports. Your friend was DUI."

"It's a lie."

"Look, Jon, you're taking this personal—"

"Damn right I am. I believe that he was murdered."

"Jon . . . please."

"His car was tampered with. I need you to find out who Frieveson Electronics in Arlington are."

"I can't do that, Jon."

"I need a favor. That's all I'm asking."

"Jon, I'm not going to do that. We have an arrangement."

"That's what I thought, too."

"But it doesn't involve personal obsessions."

"Listen to me. My friend called me as he lay dying in his car. Did you know that?"

"No, I did not."

"You know what he said?"

Meyerstein sighed. "What?"

"'They're here. And they're going to kill us all.' Those were Tiny's last words."

Silence.

"Did you hear what I said?"

The line went dead.

Seven

Reznick's mood was darkening just like the sky above North Florida. He headed off I-95 at Jacksonville and found a diner nearby. He sat down in a corner booth overlooking the parking lot, and ordered pancakes smothered in maple syrup. As he ate, he pondered his options. He still felt pangs of anger after his chat with Meyerstein. He'd been convinced she would help him.

Reznick gulped down his coffee, enjoying the caffeine fix. He began to feel more focused.

The waitress came by and refilled his cup.

"Thank you," he said.

"My pleasure, sir," she said. "You just stopping by?"

"More or less."

"You have a nice day," she said, flashing him a pearly smile before moving on to the next table.

Reznick reached into his jacket pocket for some money to pay the check, and pulled out the business card the hacker in Overtown had given him. He quickly put it away and left a twenty-dollar bill.

He went out into the parking lot and looked again at the card. Then he called the number. Three rings, and the hacker answered.

"Don't recognize this number, but I'm guessing I must know you."

"I need a favor," said Reznick.

"I don't do favors. But I recognize that voice from the other day, Jon."

"I need your help again."

"It'll cost you."

The glare from the sun was fierce. Reznick shielded his eyes.

"One thousand dollars cover it?"

"Maybe. But you'll need to do it by transferring some bitcoins to a secret account of mine. You know about Tor?"

Reznick knew the special web browser was used to access the Deep Web.

"Yeah."

A ping on his cell phone as a message came in.

"I've just sent you a one-time, computer-generated password and the account details. No one will be any the wiser. You OK with that?"

"Not a problem."

"Man, I love your attitude. It's so fucking refreshing. I need to get me some of what you're taking, right?"

Reznick didn't respond.

"So, what do you want?"

"I need everything you can get on Frieveson Electronics in Arlington, Virginia. I also want you to try and trace the following consignment number and serial number on a transceiver part."

"What the hell is that?"

"Microchip used to wirelessly communicate with a car's computer."

Reznick gave him the two numbers.

"Gimme an hour. But before you get it, you transfer the money, right?"

A soft click signaled the end of their conversation.

He headed to the diner's restroom and splashed some cold water on his face. He looked at his reflection in the mirror. Pale blue eyes stared back at him; stubble on his face. He'd always hated the unshaven look, apart from when it was necessary for a job. The look reminded him so much of his father when drinking had taken hold. The same malevolent stare. The look that said he didn't give a shit if he lived or died.

He pulled out his phone and logged onto Tor. He punched in the twenty-one-digit password and pulled up the secret bank account details. Then he paid the thousand dollars into the hacker's untraceable account via bitcoin.

He left the diner, got in his rental car, and headed north.

Just under an hour later, as he crossed into Georgia, his cell rang.

"Got something for you," the hacker said.

"Yeah? What've you got?"

"Listen to this."

"Shoot."

"The microchip in his car was part of a consignment of one thousand transceivers which had to get special documentation and clearance from the State Department before they were exported."

Reznick's senses were all switched on. "I'll need more details about the shipment."

"I'm going to find that out. But it'll take another hour and another thousand."

"You hustling me?"

"Do you want the information or not?"

"You'll get your extra thousand, my friend. But I'd better get the information I'm looking for."

"You have my word. I'll get your information by close of business."

Eight

Meyerstein stared out of her office in the Hoover Building at the storm clouds rolling across the sky over DC, still troubled by the earlier call from Reznick. She was trying to finish reading an update on the disappearance of a doomsday cult member, but her thoughts were drifting back to the incident in Miami.

Her phone rang.

"Meyerstein," she said, expecting to hear Roy Stamper on the line.

"Martha, you wanna pop through?" The voice was that of the FBI's Director, Bill O'Donoghue.

Meyerstein's heart sank. She knew what it was about.

"I'll be right there, sir."

She freshened her makeup and fixed her hair before she left her office. As soon as she arrived at the Director's office, his long-serving secretary ushered her in.

O'Donoghue was sitting behind a large mahogany desk.

"Take a seat, Martha."

Meyerstein sat down and smiled at him.

"I don't like surprises, you know," he said.

"I'm sorry, sir, I don't quite follow."

"I just got off the phone from Senator Santos from Miami, and that was after a rather terse conference call with the chief of the Miami-Dade Police."

Meyerstein inwardly braced herself, knowing what he was going to say.

"What the hell is going on down there, Martha? They're thinking the FBI sent Reznick to break into their impoundment lot."

Meyerstein knew that interagency rivalries meant that Reznick's connection with the FBI would be used to score points.

"Sir, I'd like to reassure you that—"

"I don't want reassurances, Martha, I want answers. I want to know what the hell is going on. Is that asking too much?"

Meyerstein shifted in her seat. "This is what we know. A former Delta operator who served alongside Reznick, a guy called Charles Burns, was killed in a car crash down in Miami. Wife and kid killed, too. Moments before he died, he called Reznick and said something along the lines of *they're gonna kill us all.* Accident investigation by Miami-Dade police showed he was DUI." She sighed. "Reznick believes the car was tampered with, and he broke into the impoundment lot. He called me—"

"He called you? Where the hell is he?"

"I don't know. I told him he was being irrational. Upset at his friend's death."

"What are we to make of this call to Reznick? Who was Charles Burns talking about when he said they're gonna kill us all? Was this an organized hit? And by whom?"

"We're working on that."

"Questions are being asked, Martha. And I'm going to have to answer to this."

"Sir, I'll take the flak, if that's what's required."

O'Donoghue sighed and pinched the bridge of his nose. "I'll deal with that side of things. As of now, you need to focus on finding Reznick. I can't have this guy careening around goddamn Miami or wherever he is. Miami-Dade has an APB out on Reznick. I want us to deliver him."

Meyerstein nodded. "I'll get a team together. We'll work it out, as we usually do."

"What's his next move?"

"This is Jon Reznick we're talking about. Take your pick."

"What's he been doing the last few months?"

"Reznick?" Meyerstein shrugged. "Honestly, I don't know. I don't keep tabs on him."

"Well, you should. We need to know these things. If we have a relationship with him, Martha, we need to keep him in our back pocket."

"I'll find him. We've done it before."

"Just find him. Dismissed."

Nine

Reznick was sitting in a newly stolen car in a motel parking lot in North Carolina when his phone rang.

"Mr. R., howya doin'?"

Reznick took a few moments to place the voice of the hacker. "What've you got?"

"First I want to give you a heads-up, man."

"A heads-up on what?"

"Lot of radio chatter."

"What?"

"People talking about you. Cops, Feds, you name it. They say you're wanted. They really got the hots for you."

"No kidding."

The hacker laughed. "You better watch your back, man."

"You want to get to the point?"

"Listen, I got something. Consignment details."

"And?"

"Took a lot of digging around the State Department servers. But I got it. Seems like the chips were destined for Tehran."

Reznick's mind began to race.

"Are you sure?" he asked.

"A car factory in Tehran."

Reznick could see it now. In that fleeting moment, he believed he knew what had happened. This was no accident.

"Interesting."

"You're goddamn right it's interesting. So, how the hell did it get into your dead friend's car?"

"Listen to me. You don't mention this to anyone."

"I got it."

"Tell no one."

"I hear you."

"That's us all square."

"Pleasure doing business, man . . ."

"Wait."

"You need anything else?"

"Maybe," Reznick said. "But it would involve something that might attract heat for you."

"I can look after myself. So, what do you want?"

"I want you to find someone."

"I'll need five grand before I can move on anything else. Same method."

"I'll transfer three now and two when you deliver."

"Cool. So who are you looking to find?"

"I want you to pinpoint someone, but without leaving any electronic footprints."

"I can do that."

"This is sensitive. The person I need to speak to won't be listed anywhere."

"Sounds pretty straightforward."

"She works for the FBI."

There was a pause. "This just got a helluva lot more interesting, Mr. R."

"I've got a cell phone number," said Reznick. "Now, this number, I don't want you to store it anywhere. Can I trust you on that?"

"You're the client—you get what you want. I've got a photographic memory anyway, which comes in handy."

"OK, listen to me. I want you to trace where the person that has this phone resides. It's DC, I'm sure of it, but I need to know where exactly."

A long silence before the hacker spoke. "You're not gonna kill this person, are you?"

"Shut up and listen." Reznick gave the number he had imprinted on his brain.

"We're rolling."

"How long?"

"With normal technology it would only take a few minutes. But I can see already that this cell phone is configured in a different way. It might take some time. Leave it with me."

The kid hung up.

The first thing Reznick did was pay the three thousand dollars to the hacker's account.

Thirty minutes later, Reznick was headed north.

He decided to keep on the move. He drove on in the stolen car for thirty miles, before ditching the wheels and stealing a Nissan pickup from a quiet residential street just off the freeway. It wouldn't be until dawn that the owner discovered it missing.

Ten minutes later, as he continued up I-95, his cell rang.

Reznick answered. "Yeah?"

"I've got the address."

"Give it to me."

The hacker talked slowly as he gave the address to Reznick. "Hasn't moved in three hours. Must be in the house. Residential area."

"Good work."

"Take care, man."

Ten

The first tinges of a tangerine dawn appeared on the horizon as Reznick pulled up on a tree-lined Bethesda street. He switched off the car's lights and engine. Tiredness washed over him after the long drive through the night. He stretched and popped a Dexedrine, washing it down with a can of warm Coke he'd picked up at an all-night diner en route.

He scanned the neighborhood. Large, comfortable homes in one of Washington DC's smartest suburbs.

Over the years, Reznick had visited Bethesda more times than he cared to remember. And it was always to the same place: the Walter Reed National Military Medical Center, which he knew as the Bethesda Naval Hospital.

He had lost count of the number of visits to Delta buddies who had been injured and were recuperating at the hospital. He recalled looking into the eyes of a guy he had served with—Jimmy "Mac" McCulloch, who had lost his legs when an IED detonated on the outskirts of Falluja. Tears had welled in Mac's eyes when he saw Reznick again. Reznick had just sat at his bedside, held his hand, and said a silent prayer. It was as if both of them had known words were pointless. Empty.

There had been so many others. Delta guys who had been shot up badly, bullets piercing necks, cheeks, and God knows what. But each and every one of them had faced their personal hell with a quiet courage. No histrionics.

Relatives and loved ones were another matter entirely. And he understood why. The man they'd married, the brother they'd grown up with, the son they'd raised—that person was gone. Gut-wrenching emotion spilled out each and every time they visited the hospital. The anguish. The pain. The private suffering they bore.

Reznick had been one of the lucky ones. He had returned in one piece, no limbs missing. But something else was now absent. Something that couldn't be seen. Somewhere deep inside him, a part of his soul had died. Destroyed in the carnage and blood and filth and dirt of Iraq. He'd lost too many friends.

Reznick's father had been the same. His war was Vietnam. Before, he had been outgoing, had liked a beer and to fish and hunt at weekends. But when he returned, everyone had noticed the change. The long silences. The days on end when he didn't leave his bedroom. The days when he disappeared and drank himself unconscious. The time he pressed a gun to his wife's head when she'd told him off for his drinking. It wasn't the same man who'd come back. Not the man his family had known. He'd returned home broken, consumed by guilt at living when his friends had died. But time began to heal, and his father had landed a job at a fish-packing plant in Rockland. He'd hated the work. The drudgery. The shit money. The insecurity. But he'd done it because he had to.

Reznick admired him more for that than anything else. As a boy he had watched from his bedroom window as his father returned home from working overtime after a fifteen-hour day, driving up the dirt road to their home. The car pulling to a halt, the tired look up at his son, waiting for his return.

Even after his mother died, Reznick's father didn't buckle. He came close, but he never did. He took the pain and the emptiness, and he channeled it into his shitty job. When he had time, it was fishing and hunting with his son. Teaching him to gut rabbits. Hunt deer. Fish. Shoot.

Reznick had learned it all from his father.

The sound of a door slamming shut at the house across the street snapped Reznick out of his reverie. He watched as Martha Meyerstein emerged, carrying a brown satchel and a handbag.

She opened the passenger door of her black SUV and put the bags in before walking around to open the driver's door.

Reznick got out of his car and jogged down the street, slowing down to walk up to her as she was about to get in her vehicle.

She spun around. "What the hell?"

Reznick couldn't resist a smile. "Sorry, I didn't mean to scare you."

Meyerstein shut the car door and stared at him. She clearly wasn't amused.

"What in God's name are you doing here?"

"We need to talk."

"You don't just turn up on someone's doorstep. How the hell do you know where I live?"

"I need your help."

Meyerstein gave a rueful smile. "You need my help? Jon Reznick needs my help? Do you know that the FBI are looking for you?"

"Well, they found me."

Meyerstein said nothing.

"You needed my help before. Your scientist, and the missing diplomat. I answered your call both times."

"Are you saying I'm obligated to you?"

"That's exactly what I'm saying."

Meyerstein's gaze fixed on him for a few moments. "I don't think talking this over in the middle of a goddamn Bethesda street at the crack of dawn is the time or place, Jon, do you?"

"You wanna suggest somewhere else?"

Meyerstein sighed and looked at her watch. "I've got a meeting with the Director at nine and I need to prepare."

"Look, it doesn't matter. I'll deal with it from here."

Meyerstein took a step toward him. "I just don't get you, Jon. Breaking into a secure police compound . . . Now you're outside my home. My own house, where I live with my family. This is not good, Jon. You know there's an APB out on you?"

"So arrest me."

"I don't want to arrest you."

"Help me then."

Meyerstein blinked slowly. "You've got two minutes before I need to leave. And you're on the clock. In my car—now."

Reznick got in the passenger seat of the SUV and turned to face her.

"Two main problems. Firstly, the car was going more than one hundred miles an hour and there were no skid marks."

Meyerstein said nothing.

"Secondly, I told you there was a transceiver placed in the Mercedes my friend was driving before he died. I asked you to find out more about it. But you refused. Right?"

She nodded.

"Things have moved on."

Meyerstein glanced at her watch. "One minute."

"Would it surprise you if I told you the transceiver was part of a batch destined exclusively for a foreign country?"

"So?"

"So, what if I said this foreign country was Iran?"

"OK, you've got my attention."

"Here's the thing. The transceiver is a wireless device. And it's used in all cars. But sometimes they can be modified . . ."

"Modified in what way?"

"This part was one of a thousand perfectly legally exported to Tehran. Probably to be fitted on Iranian-made cars. But I've inspected this one up close. It's been modified."

"Modified for what?"

"Modified for remote-control assassinations involving cars."

"What the hell are you talking about?"

"Boston Brakes. Heard of it?"

"Yes, I've heard of it."

"Radio-controlled assassination technique. High-end. Almost always by order from a government."

Eleven

Just after midday on the West Coast, high up in the Hollywood Hills, Jerry Morlach stood beside his pool, smoking a Cuban cigar. He stared out at the smog haze over downtown LA as the cars snaked along the freeway. He dragged heavily on the Cohiba, exhaling the smoke through his nose.

Morlach never tired of the vista. The relentless buzz of the city, day and night. A city in permanent flux. Incomers. Outsiders. Immigrants. Hustlers. Workers. And the destitute. The gangs. The shootings. The deaths. The constant movement. The fear that standing still would render a person obsolete. The uber-rich on Rodeo Drive. The flash cars. West Hollywood. The bars. The clubs. The strip joints. Sunset. The paparazzi. The cool. The wannabes. The cops. The creeps.

He thought back to his early days in the city—in the country. The late 1970s. Living hand to mouth. He had nearly starved.

By rights he should have curled up in a ball and just let the dogs chew on his bones. But he never had. He'd worked hard. He'd washed dishes at a shitty South Central diner. He'd hustled for dimes in the Valley. He'd washed cars, windows. He'd been a valet. Then he'd gotten a job in the kitchens of the Beverley Hills

Hilton. He'd washed more dishes. He'd worked his ass off. It was the American way.

He'd gone to night school to study accountancy. He spoke perfect English. He was smart. And he learned quick. He'd learned that if you want to get on, you have to be prepared to step over people on the way up. Don't stop to admire the view. It might not be there in the morning.

His big break had come when he set up his own tax consultancy in a tiny office in Century City. His client list grew and included screenwriters, directors, film scouts, and actors. Then, quite by chance, over lunch with one of his clients, who was a hot new director, Morlach had mentioned in passing that he'd read a terrific screenplay—an LA thriller—by another one of his clients. The director read it and agreed to be attached to the project, if Morlach got the funding. Within three weeks, the $15-million deal was made. The film grossed $32 million.

And so began his rise to riches as a movie producer in Los Angeles. As the years passed, he also set up his own bespoke funding company, which provided the hard cash for other producers, but only on the proviso of fifteen percent of any profits made by any film project.

The money kept rolling in. He had grown to love the city. The house. The upscale neighbors. The privacy. The luxuries only wealth could buy. The smart private schools for his children and grandchildren, the foreign holidays to Italy, the chalet in Gstaad, the jet-set friends. What was not to like?

But in truth, while the material wealth allowed him to enjoy his life, cocooned away from the smell of the streets—the sweat from immigrant labor, the stinking trash-strewn alleys—he felt empty. Bereft.

The emptiness had never left him. The soul couldn't be nourished by money. Sure, it made things bearable. Pleasant, even. But it never made him feel whole. He remembered the first time he could afford to bring his father over, three years before he'd died. His father had struggled to take it all in, and was afraid of the hustlers on Sunset Strip.

His cell phone rang, bringing him back to the present. Morlach expected it to be a producer looking for the green light on a new sci-fi blockbuster. But the caller ID was not one he recognized.

"Jerry," the voice on the line said, "we've got an urgent financing request from *people I've never met before.*" The last five words were a signal he hadn't heard in years.

Morlach took a few moments before he answered. "Do you require my signature?"

"Not at this stage. But we need you to look over the paperwork before it's issued."

Morlach dragged heavily on the cigar as the smoke filled his lungs. He knew exactly what they had in mind and his role.

"When can I expect the documentation?"

"Within the next twenty-four hours."

"Why the hurry?"

A long sigh. "We just want to ensure that we don't have any last-minute hitches and that everything is in place."

Morlach said nothing.

"So if that seems like a realistic timescale, I'll get the papers FedExed to you."

"Make it my home address."

"Very well."

"And make sure the red wax seal is on it. Is that clear?"

"Got it."

Twelve

Reznick and Meyerstein were seated at a small table in a secure room at an FBI satellite office on the outskirts of DC, with two of Meyerstein's most trusted Joint Terrorism Task Force analysts.

Meyerstein was making notes. It was going to be a long session.

The bull-necked man with a bushy mustache, who identified himself as Neil Slattery from the Department of Homeland Security, picked up an enlarged color photograph of the transceiver.

"OK, let's get this thing rolling. Let's assume for a minute that this part did come from a consignment for Iran."

"Haven't you established that yet for yourself?" said Reznick.

Slattery turned crimson. "Things take time, Jon. Firstly, I'd like to know how you know that these were shipped to Iran. And secondly, how you know this one's been modified."

"Courtesy of the State Department. Plus a little expert knowledge from my previous profession."

Slattery shifted in his seat. "Hang on, what do you mean *courtesy of the State Department?*"

"Let's just say this is a reliable source."

"Jon, you'll know better than anyone that any hint of Tehran is a red flag for us in intelligence."

Reznick nodded.

"Can you explain to those around the table, who may not be aware of this technique, how this modification could be used as part of an asymmetric terrorist threat?"

Reznick looked around the table for a few moments. "Look, I need to know that what I say stays within these walls."

"That's a given, Jon," said Meyerstein.

Reznick stared at her. "I also want a guarantee."

"What sort of guarantee?"

"If I'm going to tell you a little bit about what I know and what I've done, you need to know that some of these operations were highly classified. Unacknowledged to this day. So I can't go into details."

"Jon," said Meyerstein, "I trust everyone around this table, including you."

Reznick nodded. "This is how I see it. My friend Charles Burns was assassinated—by remote control. Made to look like an accident. For you guys who work behind a desk, I'll explain.

"The Boston Brakes method was devised by the CIA in Boston way back in the seventies, and has become more sophisticated over the years as technology has developed. It's used by intelligence agencies across the world as a way of assassinating someone without leaving a trace. So on the surface, it's made to look like an accident. A blood test then shows the person was drunk. Just like Tiny."

"How did you get hold of the police and forensic reports for Tiny's accident?" asked Meyerstein.

"The same way I got hold of the State Department intel."

"Have you carried out any Boston Brakes jobs yourself?" asked Slattery.

"I'm not going to go over things I did for this country. This isn't about me. This is about Charles Burns. It was a Brakes job. The transceivers sent to Iran—a few would've been diverted, clearly against the export license, and modified for assassination. The transceiver is fitted to the target's car. When the target is driving, the transceiver is wirelessly activated and someone remotely takes control of the car. Crashes it at top speed and the target is killed. The final autopsy report is falsified, perhaps by hackers. Everything points to a drunken and needless, tragic death."

Slattery blew out his cheeks. "That's some story, Jon."

Reznick slid the police report across the table to Slattery. "No mention of skid marks, and the photos afterward don't show any. Yet estimated speed at time of impact was over a hundred and twenty miles per hour. The fact Tiny was teetotal. The non-Mercedes part fitted to the car. It all adds up to a remote-controlled assassination."

Meyerstein leaned over, picked up the report, and flicked through it. "If someone, even if they are wrecked with alcohol, is trying to stop, there would be a skid mark as they tried to control things."

There was silence as everyone stared at Meyerstein.

A nervous cough came from Special Agent Farid Nazari, the FBI's top Iranian expert and analyst, who had remained silent until now.

"I encountered one such case a few years back," he said. "We pinpointed a military link to the suspect."

Reznick nodded. "That's where this will come from—Special Forces. Elite. Very secretive."

Nazari said, "But, if I can play devil's advocate, there is no proof that this is what actually happened. If we are to run with this and take things further, we need more than what we have."

"OK," said Meyerstein, "let's kick some hypotheticals into play. Let's just say for a minute that part of a consignment for Iran was modified by the intelligence services within Iran, and then diverted to their operatives in America for an assassination. Question is, why?"

"Why what?"

"Why Charles Burns?"

Reznick felt uncomfortable for the first time as the gazes of those around the table focused on him. "I've thought about that. There is a link."

"Jon, I trust everyone in this room. You're free to say whatever you want."

"I believe Charles was targeted. And yes, by Iranian operatives."

"But why?"

Reznick felt ill at ease. He wondered how much he could say. Or if he should even say anything about what he knew.

Meyerstein stared at him. "Jon?"

He sighed. "I think this is revenge."

"Revenge? Revenge for what?"

Reznick took a good look at the faces around the table. Intense expressions from Meyerstein and the two analysts. But there were things Reznick knew that they didn't. The sort of things that Pentagon generals knew, but were concealed from those lower down the chain. Compartmentalization.

"Do you know the last time there was a successful Iranian assassination plot on American soil?"

"Yes, I do," Meyerstein said. "Early eighties."

"Absolutely. July 22, 1980 to be precise. Iranian dissident Ali Akbar Tabatabaei was gunned down." Reznick took a deep breath and exhaled. "I believe this is retaliation . . . for an operation Charles Burns was part of, carried out six years ago."

Meyerstein looked directly at him. "Go on."

"Charles Burns was part of a team who tracked down and killed Iranian nuclear scientists."

"How do you know that?" Slattery asked.

"Because I was there. I led Charles and several other operators on these missions."

Thirteen

Everyone was quiet as Meyerstein looked around the room. She fixed her gaze on Nazari. "Farid, I don't know anyone who knows more about Iranian machinations than you. You want to jump in here?"

Nazari scratched his chin with his thumbnail. "I think we've got to be careful that we don't misinterpret things."

"Misinterpret what?" Reznick said.

"What I mean is that we don't add one and one and make five. Just because this consignment went to Iran, it doesn't mean Iranian intelligence is involved. It could be a proxy."

"True," said Meyerstein. "It's not the first time a government has been set up to look like the bad guy. False flag operations, you know the drill."

Nazari nodded. "Absolutely. It's important to keep an open mind."

"Let's look at the worst-case scenario and work back from there," continued Meyerstein. "Let's say this *was* Iranian intelligence. Give me some analysis that I can work with."

"Well, that would mean it'd come through the VEVAK, the Ministry of Intelligence and National Security." Nazari gave a sideways glance at Reznick and sighed. "Let's be clear. They are here. We all know Iranian intelligence agents live in our midst. And before you ask, I'm not one of them."

A few awkward laughs.

"We're talking people who emigrated here after the revolution, claiming asylum, but were in fact Iranian agents. And then we have those of Iranian descent who are sympathetic to the Shia cause. But whether they have anything to do with this . . . well, we're a long way from establishing that."

"But it's possible?" asked Meyerstein.

"Yes. If this is a sanctioned operation by Tehran, we've got a major problem on our hands. There's the possibility that this could be a tit-for-tat thing after the assassination of the Iranian nuclear scientists by the Delta team. And that's an unnerving prospect."

Meyerstein looked around the table. "Let's revisit two facts again. Firstly, Charles Burns called Jon, as he lay dying, and told him *they're gonna kill us all.* Secondly, Jon found out about the Tehran-bound transceivers in the car. Can this be a coincidence?" She stared at Reznick. "You said there were several of you based in Tehran, including Charles Burns."

"Yes, in and around Tehran. Three groups of two."

"I don't understand how they could know who was on that mission."

Nazari said, "That's where this theory starts running onto the rocks. There's no way they'd know that."

"Why wouldn't they know that?" said Reznick.

"For Chrissakes, it would require them accessing top-secret Pentagon files. NSA files, perhaps, on you guys."

Meyerstein shook her head in disagreement. "I think your own theory has just run onto the rocks, Farid. If Edward Snowden can access top-secret files, perhaps there are other Snowdens out there. People not in the limelight. People who haven't yet been caught."

"If I'm correct," said Reznick, "there are five others on their list, including me."

"These things don't usually appear out of thin air," said Meyerstein. "From my experience, there's chatter. Either electronic via smartphones, or through landlines, encrypted messaging." She looked at Nazari again. "Any signs?"

"Over the last six months, we have seen an uplift in messaging to various Iranians under electronic surveillance. The NSA estimates a forty-three percent increase in electronic chatter from those we are keeping tabs on. Not insignificant."

"Has that been fed into ongoing National Counterterrorism Center analysis?" asked Meyerstein.

"They're aware of the figure. A routine report was published just over a month ago—did you see it?"

Meyerstein nodded. "I was briefed on it."

"Well, for everyone who hasn't been briefed, the report concluded that, while there was a significant uplift in chatter, there was nothing to suggest anything was being planned for America. We did extensive analysis decrypting the messages, and they mostly related to Syria and Hezbollah. They also concerned geopolitical machinations with regards to us and Saudi Arabia for control of oil in the Middle East."

"And that was it?" Reznick said.

"Pretty much."

Reznick cleared his throat. "When you say *pretty much*, was there anything else which was causing concern?"

"It just had everyone scratching their heads. Some of us thought it could be disinformation." Meyerstein looked at Reznick. "Tell me about the four others."

"Why?"

"I think it's important that we assess any potential threat."

"Sure, but we need to keep this low-key."

"I don't think we're ready to equate this man's death with a possible Iranian hit squad," Nazari said. "That's my opinion. It could be a disproportionate response at this stage."

"Even knowing about the transceiver traced to an Iranian batch found in Burns's car?" Meyerstein said.

"I'm not convinced."

"But what if you're wrong? What if the Iranians have some people in play on American soil?"

"That's not their usual assassination playbook."

"But what if they're putting together an entirely new assassination playbook? Has anyone considered that?"

Fourteen

Mohsen Sazegara yawned as he peered through binoculars from behind the tinted glass of a small black Buick, parked down the street from Pete Dorfman's father's house. He was running on empty after an hour's sleep. They'd had to abandon their earlier plan to neutralize Dorfman, after some cop cars began cruising the neighborhood, following reports of a missing child. But it was only a temporary blip.

He checked his watch—9:01 a.m. He adjusted his Bluetooth headset.

"Still no sign of life," he said.

Couple of beeps in his ear. "Copy that."

Mohsen smiled. He had all the time in the world. He had been waiting for this moment for the last eighteen months, ever since his team had been assembled and given the mission. He had studied the life of Peter Dorfman. He had watched him from afar. The assassination had been aborted on three separate occasions. Each time, the abort signal had been like a dagger through his heart. He had grown to detest Dorfman.

Mohsen had followed Dorfman across Europe and now to America, observing his decadent Western lifestyle. But he sensed today was going to be the day. He could imagine Dorfman's last gasp. The look on his face for a split second as he realized how it was going to end. Dorfman wouldn't know who was responsible, why it was happening. And that in itself was rather pleasing.

"Stand by," the voice said in his ear.

Mohsen glanced in his side-view mirror as a jogger kneeled down to tie his shoelaces. The minutes dragged.

Dorfman's father had left the house over thirty minutes ago for his morning exercise with the dog. His route was the same every day: a four-and-a-half-mile power walk around the sidewalks of his quiet community.

A beep in his headset. "One and a half miles from the house."

"ETA?"

"He's stopped for a rest. You've got fifteen minutes—twenty, max. It's a green light. I repeat, this is green."

Mohsen took a moment to compose himself. He knew this was as good as it was going to get.

"Copy that." His stomach knotted. *Game on.*

He started up the car, headed farther down the street, and parked directly outside Dorfman Sr.'s house.

Mohsen pulled on his forensic gloves. Then he pulled back the slide of his Glock, checked the silencer, and put the gun in the back of his pants. It was his insurance in case things went wrong.

He leaned over and opened the glove box, then reached in and took out the military-grade stun gun—capable of dispensing a one-million-volt shock. It was disguised as a flashlight. He gripped it tight.

Mohsen picked up the backpack at his feet, took a deep breath, and opened the car door. His heart was beating hard as he walked down the garden path, shielded by palms.

He pressed the buzzer and the bell rang. Inside, footsteps padded down the hall. The door opened and the familiar face was staring back at him, eyes bloodshot. In a bizarre way, he wanted this moment to last. The frisson of anticipation.

"Peter Dorfman?" said Mohsen, giving a broad smile.

Dorfman rubbed his eyes. "Yeah?"

Mohsen smiled and pressed the stun gun to Dorfman's neck. The man's body went into spasms as he began to fit wildly. Then he collapsed backward onto the floor of the hallway, eyes wide. The adrenaline surged through Mohsen's body as Dorfman tried to crawl toward the kitchen.

Mohsen shut the door. He kneeled down beside Dorfman and pressed the stun gun to the back of his neck. "How does that feel, tough guy?" Again Dorfman began to fit violently for a few seconds. Eventually, he didn't move.

Mohsen was on the clock. He checked his watch and counted down from a minute. He then checked Dorfman's neck and wrist for a pulse. Nothing. He turned over the body and took out his iPhone. He took six shots of the corpse, and sent the photos to his handler, thousands of miles away.

He headed upstairs. He retrieved a cell phone from a bedroom and a MacBook Pro from an adjacent study, and popped them in his backpack. Then he went back downstairs.

He dragged the body down to the basement. At the bottom of the steps, he leaned Dorfman's limp body against the railings. Inside the side pocket of his backpack was a pre-tied hangman's noose. He placed it carefully around Dorfman's neck. Then he tightened it.

He threw the other end of the rope over a wooden beam and hoisted Dorfman's body up until it was hanging, limp, two feet off the ground. Then he tied the rope to the steel railings. He felt sweat on his brow.

Mohsen saw a storage box, and tipped it over under Dorfman's body to make it look as if the victim had stood on the box before he hanged himself.

Mohsen took some more shots of the hanging body.

A voice in his ear said, "Five minutes."

Mohsen put on the backpack. "*We're going home,*" he said, issuing the code words now he was ready to leave.

He headed upstairs and took one final look at the hallway where he'd killed Dorfman. He felt fantastic.

Mohsen headed out the door and into the harsh Florida sunshine, then climbed into his car and drove away.

A glance in the rearview mirror, and Mohsen saw he was smiling.

Fifteen

It had been twenty-four hours since Meyerstein's team had begun investigating the Iranian link. In the secure room, she ate in silence along with Reznick. They stared at the five names on the wall. The names were written in marker pen on a whiteboard, a red asterisk beside Charles Burns.

"Jimmy Rosen, Blaine Vincenza, Pete Dorfman, Albert Rain. Tell us about them, Jon."

"Dorfman lives in Fort Lauderdale, I know that. And Albert lives in Burlington, Vermont. I've lost touch with Jimmy and Blaine."

"We need to work through the list." Meyerstein put down the food box and stood up. "Follow me, let's take a walk."

They took the elevator to the lobby level of the office block and headed out into a courtyard with a fountain, benches, and ivy on the walls.

Meyerstein sat down as Reznick remained standing, hands in his pockets.

"I usually do my best thinking when I've got some time and space to breathe," she said. She smiled.

"You get much chance these days?"

"I'm a slave to my day planner. If it's not in there, forget it. Meetings, strategy, briefings, interviews, discussions . . ."

Reznick said nothing.

"Tell me about Charles Burns. What was he like?"

"What can I say? He was as tough as they come. Huge guy. But gentle with his wife and kid. Very respected. Didn't say a whole lot—didn't have to. We knew him as Tiny, but he was the bravest in Delta."

"I read that you extracted him from a situation in Falluja when you were in Iraq."

"Let me tell you, it wasn't pretty. But yeah, that happened. He was shot up pretty bad. They were closing in. And we know how that would've ended."

"And he was with you in Tehran?"

"Tiny rode the motorbike we used. I was on the back."

Meyerstein closed her eyes for a moment as if de-stressing. Then her cell phone rang and she picked up.

"Meyerstein." A long pause. "I need it ASAP, do you hear me, Roy?"

She ended the call and looked at Reznick.

"Problem?"

"The initial assessment of what we're facing, be it Iranians or whatever, will be with us within the hour."

"How's it shaping up?"

"We'll know soon enough."

Just over an hour later, they were back in the secure room. Slattery and Nazari had been working flat-out to track down the four other Delta operators, with limited success.

Reznick wasn't surprised. But the lack of progress only added to Meyerstein's sense of anxiety.

"I spoke to Dorfman at the funeral and afterward."

"The Special Agent in Charge of Miami is sending an agent to visit Dorfman in Fort Lauderdale. We should hear something soon."

Reznick nodded. "What about Blaine? He's the most routine and grounded of them all."

"The FBI's LA field office couldn't trace him. Anywhere. Did you know Blaine outside Delta?"

"Yeah, I knew Blaine. But I haven't seen him in over two years. Last I knew he was working as a security consultant in Hollywood. Personal security for VIPs—stars, directors, producers . . ."

"Well, we've tried tracing him, but nothing so far. He has two estranged daughters and they haven't seen him in ages."

"Chelsea and Lana."

"You know them?"

"Blaine appointed me their guardian, to look after them if something happened to him."

"So why are they estranged?"

"Blaine could never settle after leaving Delta. Wife left him, daughters sided with her."

Meyerstein sighed. "Some people never get a break."

Her phone rang and she answered it straight away. "Roy, finally . . . what's the latest?" She closed her eyes. "When?" A long silence. She ended the call and turned to face Reznick. He could tell something was wrong.

"What is it?" he asked.

Meyerstein looked at him, straight in the eyes. "Jon, I'm sorry."

"What is it?"

"The agent in Miami. She turned up at Dorfman's father's address in Fort Lauderdale. Dorfman is dead. Was found by his father. Apparently he hanged himself."

Reznick closed his eyes. "Motherfucker." He could say nothing more as he absorbed the news.

Meyerstein ran a hand through her hair. "Charles Burns in a road smash, Pete Dorfman hanged. I don't believe in coincidences."

Reznick felt sick. He turned and looked at the list of names on the board. Dark thoughts began to cloud his head.

Sixteen

Meyerstein had that familiar feeling of dread in her stomach as she sat alone in the videoconference room. The same feeling she felt when an investigation was running into trouble. But this was worse. She had ignored a warning from Reznick. A red flag. Would Dorfman still be alive if she had acted sooner?

She pushed that thought from her mind.

She was satisfied they had enough evidence to point to a link between the two deaths. She now needed to make it official, and call on all the resources available to her. Eyebrows would be raised that Reznick was back on the scene, but she could handle that.

Meyerstein stared at the huge split screen beaming multiple feeds. There were currently four people from various locations on the video call. She had listened impassively to the confirmed updates on the two sudden deaths of the ex–Delta operators.

She gathered her thoughts for a few moments, glancing at the papers in front of her before she spoke. "There is no doubt in my mind that this group of ex–Delta operators is being targeted."

Assistant Director Andrew Nuffield, in charge of the FBI's Counterterrorism Unit, said, "Martha, I agree."

Meyerstein looked up at the screen again. "This may or may not be a sanctioned Iranian operation. What is clear is that we'd be none the wiser but for Reznick's persistence. I didn't take his concerns seriously at first. I was wrong."

Nuffield nodded, as did the others.

"My ongoing concern is the other three ex-Delta operators who were on this team, alongside Jon. What has the Strategic Assessment and Analysis Unit come up with?"

"We'll have an update in less than two hours."

Meyerstein sighed heavily. "Meanwhile, these three guys who were in Tehran are at risk. We're behind the curve, and that's not a good place to be."

"Our resources and assets are being utilized to the max, Martha."

Meyerstein looked at her briefing paper on Jimmy Rosen. "Is this right? It says here that Rosen is a white supremacist in Arizona."

"That is correct. Militia nut. Loosely linked with the Hells Angels, his name has also been connected with supplying methamphetamines."

Up on the split screen, a man cleared his throat. He had short gray hair and wore a starched white shirt and dark tie. "Can I cut in here, ma'am?"

"Of course, go right ahead."

"Colonel James Seeberg, CIA, attached to the Counterterrorism Center." His piercing blue eyes stared out from the screen. "There's an element to this that we need to be very much aware of."

"And what's that, Colonel?"

"The rationale we believe for this Iranian action—if it is indeed Iranian action—is to avenge the nuclear scientists deleted by Delta operatives, am I correct?"

"Yes, that is the rationale and linkage we're working with," said Meyerstein.

"Firstly, I think we've got to be real careful about placing too much store by what Reznick asserts is true."

Meyerstein shifted in her seat. "Which part, Colonel? That his ex-Delta buddies have been assassinated? Or the operation carried out in Tehran?"

A patronizing smile from the colonel. "I think it's easy to interpret events which suit our mindset. I'm not saying that the events in Tehran didn't happen . . . it's just that I think there are implications further down the line if we do accept these events as fact."

Meyerstein shook her head. "Colonel, I don't have time for your Agency doublespeak bullshit."

"Let me apologize if I didn't make myself clear. I'm more concerned about American national interests than these four ex-Delta guys."

"Are you saying we should not concern ourselves with this?"

"Quite the opposite. I think it's important that we find them and take them to a secure place. And that includes Reznick."

"Colonel, I've worked with Jon Reznick on two separate investigations with national security implications, and his conduct and capabilities were quite exemplary. I want him part of the FBI team working with us."

"I disagree. It would be best for all concerned if Jon Reznick is taken to a secure facility with immediate effect."

"And just say he doesn't want to go, Colonel. What do you propose then?"

The colonel leaned back in his seat, unsmiling. "Assistant Director Meyerstein, that will simply not be an option for Mr. Reznick."

Meyerstein couldn't believe what she was hearing. "I'm sorry?"

FBI Counterterrorism Assistant Director Andrew Nuffield cleared his throat. "Martha, I'm with the colonel on this. We need to get Reznick out of the way. Not only for his safety, but also for national interests."

Meyerstein took a moment to absorb the full implications of what Nuffield and the others were saying. "I understand."

"It's for his own good, Martha," Colonel Seeberg said.

The faces on the split screen were impassive.

Then the colonel leaned forward, hands clasped. "I'm sorry."

"Who made this call?"

"It came from higher up the chain."

"How high?"

"Director of Homeland Security—and above."

Meyerstein fought to keep her anger in check.

"It is what it is, Martha. You need to deal with it and move on."

"Very well. If that's all, gentlemen, I have work to do."

The screen went blank, and Meyerstein sat in silence for a few seconds. She felt shock and anger course through her body.

Go with it, she thought to herself. It was what her father had taught her. *Don't let shock or anger turn to fear. Harness the energy and use it to propel yourself forward.*

"Goddamn." She ran the conversation though in her head again. She hadn't seen this coming. The idea of incarcerating Reznick against his will was unthinkable.

Meyerstein reflected on what they had said. It was the usual CIA bullshit. Colonel Seeberg didn't want any talk of American involvement in Iranian civilian assassinations to be discussed with anyone at any level, at any time.

She knew how Reznick would react. She pictured him being tasered, before being dragged out by a CIA team. She couldn't bear the thought of that. She didn't want to face up to it. But she would have to.

She would have to toe the party line on this one.

A sharp knock at the door, and Stamper walked in.

"We got a problem," he said.

"What is it?"

"It's Reznick."

Meyerstein sighed. "What now?"

"He's disappeared."

"*What?*"

"He's just stolen an FBI Lincoln from the garage and driven out onto the streets of Washington, cool as you like."

Seventeen

The first thing Reznick did was ditch the Lincoln and steal a brown Mustang from outside a diner in Dale City, just south of DC. He popped a couple of Dexedrine on the freeway and felt the chemicals rouse his system. He was switched on as he headed for Richmond, Virginia, a plan formulating in his head.

The miles on the freeway were being eaten up as he wondered what Meyerstein was thinking. He saw the way the wind was blowing. He knew the deaths of Tiny and Dorfman were connected. And he knew the Iranian connection would mean the American intelligence agencies would want him out. He knew how those agencies worked. How they thought. He knew the mission to Tehran had been top secret, and the Pentagon and CIA couldn't have a trace of it being divulged in any form.

He knew the CIA would claim they wanted to keep him safe at a secure facility. He knew that was bullshit. It was just what was in American interests. And to hell with anyone else. They would take him off the case—keep him against his will at a military base. Or, if need be, kill him.

Did Meyerstein see this? The Feds didn't always know what the CIA got up to. One thing Reznick did know was he sure as hell wasn't going to sit around and let another Delta buddy die. Especially not Blaine. He thought of his kids and the vow he'd made.

He needed to be alert. He couldn't be predictable. He knew they would be looking for him everywhere. Slowly, as the miles ticked by, the plan started to take shape. Crystallize.

He figured a car journey to the West Coast would take a day and a half without sleep. And it would mean a number of stolen cars, increasing the risk of getting caught. The airports and train stations in and around DC, including Baltimore, would be targeted.

Richmond was only two hours south of DC, and had an international airport with multiple destinations. He was going to hop on a flight. He had fake documentation already prepared for such emergencies. He just needed somewhere far enough away from LA, but close enough to drive there in a few hours . . .

Just before two o'clock, he parked up at a garage opposite the terminal building at Richmond International Airport. He went to the bathroom and into a stall, where he ripped open the lining of his jacket and pulled out two thousand dollars in cash, along with a fake passport, two fake credit cards, and a fake driving license—all under the name Ronald Barr.

Reznick ate a slice of pizza inside the terminal while he looked at the flight boards. New York, Los Angeles, Boston, Miami, and . . . Las Vegas.

He bought a ticket for a Delta flight, leaving at 4:45 p.m.

He got in line, was frisked by security, and answered some dumb-ass questions from an official before he was ushered into coach class.

Once on board and seated, Reznick closed his eyes and drifted off to sleep.

It was dark when he left the terminal at Las Vegas in the hired Chevrolet Camaro and headed off into the desert night. He cranked up the air con. Just before midnight, he stopped off in Baker in the Mojave Desert for a beer and to stretch his legs. A huge thermometer in the deserted town showed it was 91 degrees. His shirt was sticking to him.

Reznick went into the bar, a country song playing in the background. Two old guys playing pool, Fox News on with the volume down.

"Heineken," he said.

The bartender handed over a chilled bottle of beer, and Reznick sat down on a stool.

"Hard day, honey?" she asked.

Reznick glanced up at the TV, which showed firefighters fighting fierce blazes near Los Angeles. He took a couple of gulps of his drink. It felt good. "Had worse."

"Where you headed at this time of night? You going to Vegas? Because if you are, I'd love a ride."

"Sorry, opposite direction."

"I love LA. You ever been there, honey?"

"Couple times."

"Had a lot of fun times in LA, let me tell you."

Reznick gulped the rest of the beer, quenching his thirst. "Is that right?"

"Lot of fun." She pointed up at the TV. "Don't worry, that's away in the San Gabriel Mountains, above Azusa. I take it you're not going there."

Reznick pushed the empty beer bottle toward her. "Same again."

She got another from the fridge, prized off the metal top, and handed it to him.

Reznick gave her twenty dollars. "Keep the change."

"Thank you." She smiled.

The TV flashed up a picture of Blaine. Reznick pointed at the screen. "You wanna turn that up?"

She cranked up the volume. "Sure thing."

The newsreader's voice said, "*The missing man is a Hollywood security consultant, Blaine Vincenza. Police are concerned for his safety and have asked Mr. Vincenza to contact them at the earliest opportunity, as his family fear for his well-being. He may need medication for a heart condition.*"

Reznick stood up. "Gotta go."

"You not staying for another?"

Reznick was already thinking ahead. "Maybe another time."

"Take care, honey."

Reznick headed out of the cool bar into the stifling desert night. He got back in the hire car and headed west. His next stop: Los Angeles.

Eighteen

"We got something!" Stamper shouted across the command room, on the fifth floor of FBI Headquarters.

Meyerstein rubbed her eyes and stared up at the image of Reznick on the big screen. "We're sure this is him?"

Stamper nodded. "This is the one and only Jon Reznick, disembarking from a Delta flight from Richmond, and walking the arrivals hall at McCarron International, Las Vegas, three hours ago."

Meyerstein shook her head. "How the hell did we allow him to get this far?"

"Blindsided us again, Martha. We had to prioritize. Dulles and Reagan International were covered, not to mention Baltimore. The biggies . . . The obvious choices."

"He'll be headed for LA."

Stamper nodded.

"What've we got in place?"

"LA field office is on this, as is Vegas."

Meyerstein's phone rang and she picked up.

"Ma'am, Special Agent Thomas Clarkson. We have something on Reznick."

Meyerstein knew Clarkson, a smart rookie who worked on the fourth floor.

"We've already got the Vegas lead, Thomas."

"We now know what car he's driving. It's a Chevrolet Camaro."

"Where did he pick it up?"

"Avis rental at McCarron. License plate is being circulated. He's using false ID. The name's Ronald Barr."

Meyerstein closed her eyes and shook her head. "Goddamn. OK, Thomas, good work. Feed this into all US intelligence agencies. We need to find him."

"Will do, ma'am."

Meyerstein ended the call and relayed the news to Stamper. "Is he trying to contact Vincenza himself?"

Stamper said nothing.

"What is it?"

"We could do without this, Martha."

"Tell me about it."

"We're being made to look stupid."

"OK, Roy, I get the picture."

"What's he playing at?" Stamper said. "He needs to keep the hell out the way."

"Roy, I said I get the picture."

"Martha, how many times do you have to defend Reznick? He's getting in the way."

"Look, I know this isn't ideal. But I think he'll be in touch with us again to work this case."

"Martha, this is wrong. Langley doesn't like this guy. They think he's getting favorable treatment from you. Any deal with him we cut in the past is over. We need to move on."

"What the hell does that mean?"

"I'm saying we need to cut our ties with Reznick once and for all."

"And why would we do that? Hasn't he been invaluable in the past?"

Stamper shook his head. "Martha, you're reading this wrong."

"I'm reading this wrong. How am I reading this wrong?"

"I think this time he's gone too far. I think he's at odds with what we're about."

Meyerstein stared at him silently.

Stamper frowned. "What?"

"Next time you start questioning my judgment, we're going to have a discussion about a future posting for you. Do you understand me?"

Stamper flushed as Meyerstein's phone began to ring.

She stared at him. "Did you hear what I said?"

"Loud and clear."

"Get to it, then. Find me Reznick."

Stamper left the room and she answered her phone. "Meyerstein."

"Martha, it's O'Donoghue."

She was surprised he was still awake.

"Sir, what can I do for you?"

"Martha, I just got out of a meeting with the Director of the CIA, and this Iranian thing has got them spooked."

She said nothing.

"What is also worrying them is Reznick."

"Sir, I think—"

"Hold on. I think it would be in everyone's interests if he's found and taken to a secure location. Do you understand?"

"With respect, sir, I don't agree."

"What do you mean you don't agree? I'm giving you a direct order."

"Sir, I think the reason Reznick took matters into his own hands was because he knew what we had in store for him. And I think he's useful on the outside, leading us to Vincenza and the Iranians."

"Martha, you're too close to this. What's apparent is that you're losing control of the situation."

Meyerstein bristled at his words. "Sir, give me forty-eight hours and I'll have this cleaned up."

A long sigh. "We want Reznick out of the way."

"And I'm saying, sir, let me deal with this."

"What's the latest?"

"Reznick is on the move. Headed to Los Angeles. False name. But I've got a proposition for you."

"I'm listening."

Meyerstein was feeling more and more annoyed by his tone. "What I propose is that I head to LA and make contact with Reznick myself. That's where it's going to play out."

There was a long silence before O'Donoghue spoke.

"OK, forty-eight hours."

Nineteen

In a rundown part of East Los Angeles, the morning sun peeked through a gap in the shabby houses, dusty palm trees hanging limp in the dead air. Reznick was sitting in a parked car opposite a boxing gym, drinking a double espresso. He watched as an old man opened up the gym's door and went inside.

Reznick waited a couple of minutes before getting out of the car and following the man inside. He could hear footsteps on the floor above. He headed up a flight of stairs to a hallway, photos of boxers on the walls. He noticed a few black-and-white shots of Roberto Durán, the Panamanian brawler—one of the greatest boxers ever. A guy raised in the slums of El Chorrillo. A fighter Reznick's father had admired. *Manos de Piedra* . . . Hands of Stone. A man who'd win at all costs. Reznick remembered his father reading boxing articles about Durán to him when he was a boy. He had listened intently, and admired Durán's almost monastic dedication. Unbowed, and mostly unconquered.

Farther down the corridor he noticed a set of stairs leading down. As Reznick entered the spacious gym at the bottom, the old man turned around, rheumy brown eyes creasing up.

"Can I help you, son?"

"Looking for a friend of mine."

"What kind of friend?"

"Way back in the day. He learned to box here. Little white kid. Blaine."

A smile washed over the man's leathery face. "Blaine? You kidding me? You one of Blaine's friends?"

Reznick nodded.

"Man, that was a long time ago."

"I believe he still comes back here. Recruits the guys from the gym for security jobs he has."

The man was quiet for a few moments. "You're asking a lot of questions. Why you want to speak to him?"

"Listen, old man, can you help me or not?"

"You box?"

"I have boxed."

"When?"

"In the Marines."

The old man grinned. "You get your ass kicked?"

"Not too often."

The old man sighed. "Not seen Blaine for a couple of weeks."

"I believe his mother still lives around here."

"Not anymore. He moved his momma away. Neighborhood getting too crazy. Shame really. I remember the day Mrs. Vincenza brought Blaine in. He was getting pushed around. White kid among a lot of Hispanic guys. Can be tough."

Reznick said nothing, happy to let the man talk.

"His mother was a nice lady. Lost her husband in Lebanon. And she wanted her son to get toughened up."

"You must've done a pretty good job," said Reznick.

"This is a proper boxing gym, son."

Reznick looked around at the walls, the pictures of tough local fighters. "So I see."

"Listen, you know LA at all?"

"Some."

"A lot of the guys that Blaine hires are for close protection work for big shots. Bit of muscle for premieres and after-parties. The guy who runs some of the operations is one of my old fighters, Pedro Mendes."

"Where can I find Pedro?"

The old man pointed behind him. "Ask him yourself."

Reznick turned around and saw a little guy, impossibly lean, with veins bulging out of his neck.

Dark brown eyes fixed on him. "What you want?"

"I'm a friend of Blaine's. I was told you might be able to help."

Mendes shrugged. "Who are you? You a cop?"

"Ex-Delta."

Mendes cocked his head to one side. "You don't look ex-Delta to me. Look like one of those candy-ass boys from West Hollywood." He grinned like a jackal.

Reznick stared back at him. "How old are you?"

"Fuck is it to do with you? Come in here asking about Blaine? I don't know you. I don't give a fuck about you." Mendes stared at him, nerves twitching. "This is where real boxers are made."

"I'm sure you can box. But I'm not sure you can fight. You wanna see the difference?"

Mendes spat on the floor and glared. "You do a lot of talking, don't you?"

He stood, snarling. He was about six or seven yards from Reznick. Then he rushed forward and tried a hook with his right.

Reznick slammed his left forearm into the neck of the oncoming boxer. Mendes dropped to the ground, out cold. Reznick had hit the carotid sinus.

He picked up the unconscious Mendes and slapped him a few times around the face. The boxer came to, eyes rolled back in his head.

Reznick grabbed his neck and the man winced. "OK, here's how it's gonna work, Pedro. I'm an old friend of Blaine's, and I'm trying to reach him. Where can I find him?"

Mendes shook his head and Reznick squeezed tight.

He winced. "OK . . ."

Reznick loosened his grip. "Speak."

"He occasionally has lunch at a restaurant in Studio City."

"I don't want *occasionally*. I'm not interested in *occasionally*. I want to know where to find him."

"OK. Every night he dines at the same place."

"Every night?"

"Every night."

"What's the name of the restaurant?"

"Nobu in Malibu. Where all the big stars go."

"What does he drive?"

"Ferrari. Black."

Reznick frowned. "Doesn't sound like Blaine's sort of place—or car."

"He moves with a lot of interesting people these days. He likes to be seen out and about and with the right set of wheels."

Reznick grabbed the guy by the throat again. "Don't fuck with me. If you're not telling the truth, I know where to find you. Do you understand?"

The guy nodded, eyes closed tight as Reznick pressed into his windpipe.

Reznick released him, and Mendes coughed and spluttered. Reznick turned to the old man. "Appreciate that."

Then he headed out onto the streets, as the harsh LA sun began to beat down.

Twenty

Just after noon, Jerry Morlach was escorted to a corner table on the sun-drenched roof terrace of Soho House in West Hollywood. The private members' club was located high above Sunset Boulevard, on the top two floors of a high-rise. He was lunching with a French arthouse producer with a rumored penchant for cocaine, hookers, and any starlets who crossed his path.

Morlach smiled as his lunch guest arrived. The producer ordered a bottle of Chablis and a salad, while Morlach stuck with his usual steak—rare—washed down with a Perrier. Morlach listened patiently as the producer talked incessantly, rubbed his nose frequently, and visited the restroom on four separate occasions.

Morlach took it in his stride. He stared out at the downtown skyscrapers in the distance. He had seen it all in the last twenty-five years, mixing with the movers and shakers of Hollywood. He didn't give a damn about movies. He didn't give a damn about art. He just cared about the money. He needed big returns—his clients demanded it. Their money had to be invested in surefire winners. Blockbusters. Big-name summer hits. But he had also seen that arthouse and indie films could provide a spectacular return for a modest outlay, so he always took the meetings.

Morlach's mind wandered as the Frenchman got more animated, talking about the *struggle* and *basic conflict* of the characters, which he insisted were vital to great cinema. Morlach let the producer drone on as his thoughts turned to the mysterious call he'd received, alerting him to yesterday's delivery. The documentation had been postmarked Dubai, but this concealed the true geographical origin of the package. He knew what was inside and the intended purpose. He just didn't know who would collect or when.

He sipped more water as the Frenchman prattled on. Morlach endured the lunch for another painful hour before he ordered another bottle of Chablis, to the delight of the producer. Then he picked up the check and left, alone.

After descending the private elevator to the parking garage, he was about to start up his car when his cell phone rang.

Morlach answered on the third ring. "Yeah," he said, clearing his throat.

A beat. "Good lunch?" The voice was the same as yesterday.

Morlach groaned. "Interminable, if you must know."

"He's very talented, they say."

Morlach said nothing.

"I believe there was a safe delivery."

"It's all in order—got it yesterday. Is there anything else I should do?"

A long sigh. "We have a fast-moving situation."

"I need to know more."

"Don't stray far from home in the next forty-eight hours."

"Why not?"

Silence.

"I said, why not?"

"Plans have been altered."

"*Altered?*"

"They've run into a few snags. Hence the new documentation. And they'll pick it up in person."

"No problem at all. Whatever you require, I will assist."

Twenty-One

The sky was burnt orange as Reznick headed west on the Pacific Coast Highway. The smell of the salty air reminded Reznick of home, by the cove in Maine. He had always loved the sea. The ever-changing vista . . . the breakers crashing onto the shoreline. It made him feel free.

Reznick saw a sign for the restaurant up ahead. He drove past for a couple of miles to make sure no one was following him, before turning around and heading back into Malibu. He pulled into the parking lot of a McDonald's and switched off the engine. Nobu was opposite, on the ocean side of the freeway.

He pulled out his binoculars and looked across at the entrance to the restaurant. He didn't know for sure if Blaine would be at the restaurant tonight, but it was his best shot.

Reznick watched and waited. He felt his stomach rumble from lack of food. He couldn't remember the last time he'd eaten. He went inside the McDonald's and ordered a burger, fries, and large Coke, then sat by the window and stared across at the fancy cars pulling into Nobu's private parking lot. After finishing his food, he went to the restroom and popped a couple of Dexedrine. He felt alive again.

Reznick returned to his car and resumed his stakeout. He replayed the call from Tiny in his head. He thought of Pete Dorfman, drinking on the roof terrace in South Beach. Both men's lives snuffed out as methodically and clinically as the scientists' lives Reznick and his Delta crew had snuffed out. And now it was retribution time.

The minutes dragged into hours. Still nothing. Reznick wondered if the punk at the boxing gym hadn't played him. It was a possibility. But he had to find Blaine and warn him of the threat.

Just then, a sleek black Ferrari cruised into view and turned into the Nobu parking lot. The car light went off, the driver's door opened, and Blaine stepped out, buttoning his blazer over his white shirt. He looked every inch the affluent West Coast businessman as he entered the exclusive restaurant.

Reznick waited for a few moments. The quickest way to get to the restaurant was to jaywalk across the busy freeway. But just as he moved to get out of the car, a Ducati motorbike pulled up outside Nobu. A helmeted passenger climbed off the pillion seat and opened up the backpack of the man riding the bike.

A feeling of dread came over Reznick. He sensed something was wrong. Badly wrong.

"No, no . . ." he said out loud, as he realized in that instant something was definitely going down.

The passenger pulled out a small metal device and placed it underneath the Ferrari. He then climbed back on the bike, which was gunned hard, and disappeared into the steady Pacific Coast Highway traffic.

They had taken less than thirty seconds to plant the device, and no one but Reznick had witnessed it.

Twenty-Two

Reznick slammed the car into reverse and cut across the highway, swerving to avoid an oncoming truck as he gave chase. He pulled up the number for Nobu on his phone, heart pounding as he peered ahead at the traffic. Through the myriad of lights he picked out the motorbike, tearing west up the coast road.

The restaurant's phone rang. And rang.

Eight rings later, someone picked up.

"Nobu Malibu, good evening."

"I need to speak to the manager," Reznick said, raising his voice above the roar of the engine.

"I'm sorry, the manager isn't available just now. How can I help?"

"Who am I speaking to?"

"Heidi Franzen, duty restaurant supervisor, sir."

"Heidi, I need to speak to a customer of yours—Blaine Vincenza. He just arrived a few minutes ago."

"Sir, I'm afraid I'm not at liberty to discuss who is or isn't dining with us this evening. If you'd like to leave your number—"

"Heidi, I haven't got much time. I need to speak to Blaine right now."

"Sir, with respect, I don't know who you are."

"My name is Jon Reznick."

"Mr. Reznick, it's not our policy to—"

"Listen, Miss whatever-your-name-is, I don't give a damn about your policies."

"Sir, I'm sorry, we're very busy this evening—"

"Heidi, do you want me to spell it out for you? There's a fucking bomb under Blaine's black Ferrari, outside your goddamn restaurant. So are you going to—"

She hung up.

Reznick thought of Blaine and the other diners inside, oblivious.

"Fuck."

Thoughts were tearing through his head.

His cell phone rang, barely audible as the traffic roared past in the other direction. He didn't recognize the number.

"Yeah, who's this?"

"Don't hang up." Meyerstein's voice. "Jon, we've got an approximate fix on your location."

Reznick took a few moments to think of his next move. "How did you find me?"

"When you use the word *bomb*—and a few sentences earlier, *Jon Reznick*—it's picked up by the NSA."

"Nice to know the NSA is respecting an American's privacy."

"You're in Malibu, aren't you?"

"I'm heading away from Malibu. And I just want to let you know that you've got a problem. A big fucking problem."

"Tell me about this bomb."

"Two guys on a motorbike pulled up outside Nobu about two minutes ago, and placed what looked like a magnetic bomb on the underside of Blaine Vincenza's black Ferrari."

A pause. "Blaine? Ex-Delta Blaine?"

"The very one."

"Copy that."

"Listen, you need to clear the restaurant. You need to get Blaine. No one touches that Ferrari."

"Got you."

Reznick swerved as he overtook a truck, narrowly avoiding clipping another car.

"Jon, we have a chopper in the air now. An FBI SWAT team is five minutes behind you. Have you got a visual on the bike?"

"Affirmative. But my car is no match. I'm barely keeping up. Listen, you need to seal off that restaurant."

"Myself and the bomb squad are on that, Jon."

Reznick braked hard as a pickup truck cut in front of him.

"Goddamn!"

"Are you OK?"

"Fucking Californian drivers, that's all."

Meyerstein sighed. "Support is only a minute behind you, and closing fast."

"Anti-jamming signals would be first port of call for bomb squad. Could be triggered by cell phone."

The sound of a radio crackling in the background.

Meyerstein said, "Hang on. Bomb squad's ETA is four minutes."

"Where are you?"

"I'll be there in less than a minute . . . " The line began to break up. "What about you, Jon?"

Reznick stared at the road ahead as the motorbike headed off into the hills outside Malibu. "Looks like these guys are heading off the highway. I'll be in touch."

"Be careful, Jon."

Then she hung up.

Twenty-Three

Mohsen Sazegara was watching the Nobu parking lot through military binoculars, from the upper deck of the safe house, high up in the Malibu hills. Police cruisers had sealed off the entrance, and no one was getting in or out.

He adjusted his Bluetooth headset and turned to his brother. "I don't like this. Something's been compromised."

"Let's roll with it, Mohsen," said Behzad.

Mohsen watched a black Suburban pull up at the cordon. Four men wearing dark suits got out, followed by a woman.

"Hang on . . . who's this, Behzad?"

Behzad, the computer specialist within the team, took dozens of photos with his telephoto lens. Then he pulled out the SD card from the camera and slid it into the side of his MacBook Pro.

"Give me a moment. I'll scan against our database."

"These are not ordinary cops."

"Everyone who is anyone in the American intelligence community is on our system," said Behzad.

"What about Vincenza and Reznick? They're not on it."

"We have their details from other sources." Moments later, Behzad smiled. "Well, well, well," he said, and flipped the laptop around so Mohsen could see what he'd found.

Mohsen stared at a photo of an attractive woman who looked in her late thirties.

"Who is she?"

"FBI Assistant Director Martha Meyerstein. It says here that she's worked with Reznick in the past."

Mohsen grinned. "You kidding me? An assistant director? And Vincenza inside?"

"The orders were very clear. Strictly ex-Delta only, Mohsen. You know that."

Mohsen stared through the viewfinder of the binoculars. "I know what the orders were. I also know that if we do something more direct, high-value casualties such as this Meyerstein woman are not a problem. We're sending them a message, aren't we?"

Behzad went to the front of the deck and stared through his telescopic lens. "We've got a window of opportunity, Mohsen. But Meyerstein is not on the list."

Mohsen stared down at the gathering Feds. Then his attention was drawn to police cars farther down the Pacific Coast Highway, sirens on and lights flashing. He trained his binoculars on the fast-moving vehicles. He wanted to get Vincenza.

"They're locking it down. Shit," he said.

"How long have we got?"

"Anything from five to seven minutes."

"That gives us just enough time for Vincenza."

Mohsen said nothing.

"They're onto us, Mohsen. We can't jeopardize the mission."

"You might be right. Damn." Mohsen dialed the number of his handler. "I need to speak to our friend in Mexico. Right now."

"Leave it with me," the handler said, and hung up.

A minute later, Mohsen's phone rang. He didn't recognize the caller ID.

"Who's this?"

"Is this a secure line?" The gravelly voice belonged to Jorge Garcia, the infamous head of the Tijuana Cartel.

"Sure. Thanks for calling back so quick."

"We have a deal, don't we? And I should say, thank you for the equipment. Very nice gift." He was referring to the half-dozen Misagh 2 weapons—the Iranian shoulder-launch, surface-to-air missiles—that his group had delivered six months earlier. "We hope we can repay you in the future."

"I'm calling in the favor right now."

"Just name it."

"Rosario is working with some of my friends in Arizona, right?"

"That's correct, my friend."

"When she's finished, we might need her for a Plan B we could be looking at. We might need to leave California in the very near future. Our first choice is via plane. But that might change, do you follow me?"

"We got that covered. Leave it with me. We'll get the vehicles readied. And any logistics. Rosario will not let you down, I promise."

"Can I call I call you on this number if I need to speak to you direct?"

"Count on it. Best of luck, my friend. And I look forward to hearing from you again."

The line went dead.

Mohsen relayed the details of the call to his brother.

Behzad said, "I think we should pick up our papers, get the hell out of here, and regroup."

Mohsen smiled. "Jorge is a good guy. He has our back."

"I'm not doubting that. But I don't like that the Feds have just turned up. This is not good. They're on to us."

"Maybe."

Mohsen trained the binoculars back on the Nobu parking lot. At that moment, Mohsen saw a man emerge from the restaurant.

"Hang on a minute," he said. "We have something. Vincenza and Meyerstein are talking, you see them?"

"Got it."

"We have them both in our sights." He turned to look at his brother. "Very tempting, wouldn't you say?"

"You want to kill them both?"

Mohsen smiled. "Why not?"

Twenty-Four

Reznick was driving hard as he headed up Malibu Canyon Road, struggling to keep up with the lights of the bike in the distance. He heard his cell ring over his Bluetooth headset.

"Talk to me, Jon." Meyerstein's voice was tight.

"Where the hell is the chopper? I'm following these guys up into the hills. I don't know where the fuck I'm going."

"Mechanical problem. It had to turn back."

"Are you kidding me?"

"We've got two mobile SWAT teams on the way. They're not far behind."

"Tell them to get a move on. This car is a heap of junk."

The signal dropped and they were cut off.

"Fuck."

Reznick was gaining on the bike as they moved inland. Up ahead, he saw the lights weave through the canyon. He wondered if the guys on the motorbike thought they'd lost him.

His thoughts went back to the bike's arrival, and the location. The restaurant was right beside the ocean. But on the other side were the hills, and their winding roads and houses, overlooking the ocean from on high.

Line of sight.

The realization crashed through his head like a concrete block.

His foot pressed to the floor as he drove higher into the dark hills, headlights illuminating the winding canyon road.

His cell rang.

"Jon, are you there?"

"Yeah, I'm on it. Listen, you've got a major problem."

"I think I'm aware of that, Jon."

"I'm not talking about the team that laid the bomb."

"What then?"

"You're being watched. Right now." A coyote ran across the road. Reznick swerved, narrowly avoiding it. "Goddamn."

"You OK?"

"Fucking Californian wildlife."

"So tell me . . . where might they be watching us from?"

"Hills directly above Malibu. Hundreds of homes there with direct line of sight."

"So how—"

"Never mind how. You need to make the bomb safe, as they may remote detonate at any time. Listen to me—"

The signal dropped off again, killing the call.

Reznick sped on through the canyon. Around the sheer drops of the hillside roads. All the time, in the distance, the single light from the motorbike. Then he saw a sign for Las Virgenes Canyon Road. Up ahead, the bike started to pull farther away and then hung a right onto Mulholland Highway.

He tried to accelerate but the vehicle was struggling on the steep incline. He was barely doing sixty-five.

Blue flashing lights appeared in his rearview mirror. He glanced behind and saw two motorcycle cops tearing toward him, lights on full, sirens blaring.

"Gimme a fuckin' break."

Reznick's heart sank as they got closer. He waited for them to cut him off. But instead, they tore on past on their high-powered bikes. Dust kicked onto Reznick's windshield.

His cell phone rang again. It was Meyerstein.

"Who the hell sent up the motorbike cops?"

"Jon, second chopper is now finally in the air. SWAT's going to be with you in no time."

"There is no time. Listen to me—the California Highway Patrol is no match for these guys who planted the sticky. They need to track them, but not get too close."

"Jon, the two officers are both armed and highly trained."

"Meyerstein, you're not getting this. This is not a straightforward shoot-out with some bad guys. These are pros. They'll devour those cops if they're stopped, I can guarantee that. Hold on . . ."

Reznick sped around a tight bend as he approached the turn for Mulholland Highway. He gripped the steering wheel tight, struggling to stay on the road as it snaked through the canyon.

A mile or so up ahead, through the scrub, he saw blue lights flashing.

He pressed on along Mulholland, the lights of Malibu down the mountains, away in the distance.

Meyerstein's voice came back through his headset. "Jon, the guys have been pulled over . . ."

The cell signal seemed to drop again and Reznick groaned.

"Shit . . ."

"What is it?" Reznick asked.

"Goddamn signal keeps dropping."

Reznick turned a corner and caught sight of the blue police lights again. "Got them. They've pulled them over at an overlook."

"Copy that, Jon."

The cell signal cut out once more.

Reznick drove on, fast. A couple of minutes later, he headed around another bend and saw the two BMW cop bikes at the side of the road.

But where were the cops?

He pulled over by the overlook, beside some overgrown shrubbery, and got out of the car. There was blood on the ground.

Shit.

The car's headlights showed the soles of a pair of black leather boots sticking out from the trees. He went over and kneeled down. The body of a dead cop, two bullets drilled into the forehead.

His mind flashed back to Tiny's last words. *They're gonna kill us all.*

He headed over to the cops' motorbikes. It was then he saw the second cop, lying face down. Dead. There was no sign of the guys who'd planted the bomb.

Reznick stood and contemplated his next move. Making up his mind, he bent down, took a gun from the cop's holster, and climbed on one of the bikes, revving the engine.

A police dispatcher's voice came over the radio. "Echo Five Delta, respond."

Reznick picked up. "Two officers shot dead. My name is Reznick. Refer to Assistant Director Meyerstein of the FBI. I repeat, two officers have been shot dead. I'm on it."

"Echo Five—"

"Shut the fuck up. Assailants on Ducati bike. I'm more than two miles behind, heading north on Mulholland. Weapon used was a 9mm handgun, point blank." Reznick kicked the bike into first gear and sped away, clicking through the gears until he was hitting ninety.

A crackle down the line. "Please identify yourself, Officer."

Reznick switched off the radio. The wind buffeted him as the bike weaved and accelerated along Mulholland. He saw a truck and overtook it at breakneck speed. Then he saw a sign for Calabasas. He powered through the small town and farther into the hills.

He couldn't see the bike.

His mind raced. Had he lost them? Had they disappeared onto a side street in Calabasas?

A few minutes later, Reznick was snaking down Old Topanga Canyon Road, back toward Malibu. The lights of the hillside houses and the communities of the canyon were all around him.

Reznick spotted more lights up ahead, half a mile or so. The bike had stopped at an overlook. He rounded a bend and felt his heart race as he sped down the hillside highway, the smell of oak trees and burnt vegetation hanging in the balmy air.

The headlights of a truck heading up Topanga illuminated the overlook. The bike was there. No passengers in sight.

Reznick slowed down, moving down the gears, and edged the police bike beside the Ducati. He got off and stared out at a dirt trail. Then he turned and saw something in the distance. Two silhouettes heading across the dark canyon.

He took his cell from his shirt pocket and dialed Meyerstein's number.

"Listen up," he said, "there's an overlook halfway down Topanga. The two guys have dumped the Ducati. I'm in pursuit on foot."

He pulled his Beretta from his waistband and headed down the hillside toward the two figures.

On the line, someone cleared their throat.

"Jon." The voice of Meyerstein. "Jon . . . we've got your location."

Reznick headed into the undergrowth and fought his way through overhanging branches and overgrown vegetation. When he got onto the dirt trail he began to run. Fast. Heart pounding. The full moon shone on the two figures in the distance as they moved east.

He was getting closer. Two hundred yards. Then one hundred and fifty. Then one hundred.

He began to hear them panting.

Reznick trained his gun on them. "Freeze!"

The men stopped dead in their tracks.

"Hands on your head! Now!"

Reznick moved closer. "Do not fucking move or I will blow your fucking brains out!"

Whispers in Persian. "*Say nothing. Do you hear me? Tell the American nothing.*"

Reznick sensed something was wrong. He stepped forward, until he was six or seven paces away from them. The moonlight bathed the verdant canyon in an eerie light.

"Very slowly, turn around, hands on head. One wrong move, you die."

The two men turned around and faced him. Young kids. Iranians. The fuckers who had planted the sticky on Blaine's car.

Reznick thought they seemed distracted, eyes darting this way and that.

"Move, and you die," he said.

Suddenly, a green tracer light fixed on one of their foreheads.

Reznick spun around. He saw a spectral figure in the distance. Then two shots rang out.

Twenty-Five

Meyerstein was sitting in the back of a mobile command center in the Nobu parking lot, watching night-vision footage from the police chopper circling over the two bodies. She watched as Reznick was cuffed by the FBI SWAT team leader and looked up toward the chopper. Her heart sank as he was led back to Mulholland.

Meyerstein looked over at Roy Stamper. "So I'm assuming we're talking at least two Iranian cells on the go, right?"

"Counterterrorism are running all the angles on this. I need to level with you, Martha. The last thing we need is for Reznick to be involved. Look at the results."

"That's enough!"

"We wanted to bring those guys in. We needed to speak to them. No goddamn use now, Martha."

"Jon Reznick didn't kill them! He was the one who managed to track down his old buddy. He was the one who witnessed them planting the bomb, and warned us we were being watched. We don't know who took these guys out."

"Martha, we've had this chat before. But I'll say it again—Reznick is trouble. He doesn't play by our rules. He doesn't adhere to the rule of law."

Meyerstein glanced at a screen, which showed a bomb technician's truck pulling up beside the Ferrari. Two bomb disposal guys got out and were briefed by one of Stamper's men. Then they peeked under the Ferrari with flashlights and mirrors.

A couple of minutes later, there was a new voice on Meyerstein's radio.

"Special Agent Luke Farmer, LA field office bomb technician."

"Go ahead," Meyerstein said.

"Ma'am, it's a tilt trigger mechanism. Very neatly put together. But it's also cell phone activated."

"What about the timer?"

"No timer . . . we're sure of that."

"How long until you make it safe?"

"If you mean how long until we're able to extricate the actual device, probably the rest of the night. But as long as no one sits in the car, we'll be fine."

Meyerstein thought the technician sounded unduly confident, but told him to get to it. Her natural instinct was to err on the side of caution. She would much rather have doom-laden predictions for an operation so plans could be made accordingly. She was suspicious of certainty. Her father, a leading Chicago litigator, had warned her of that many times. *Just when you think you have it all figured out, something comes out of the blue to wreck the best-laid plans.* She could hear his brash voice now.

She turned to Stamper. "Where's Vincenza now?"

"He's gone back into the restaurant. Refusing to talk to us."

Meyerstein sighed. "Unbelievable."

"You want me to go in and sort it out?"

She shook her head. "Leave him to me. I'll deal with him."

Twenty-Six

Mohsen Sazegara stared through the powerful military binoculars he was holding in his right hand. In his left, he held a prototype radio-frequency meter. He looked at the readings and saw the spectrum that had been blanked out by the jammers.

He smiled. Little did the Feds know that his team had the latest technology, designed specifically to evade the finest American countersurveillance methods available to the FBI. They also had the advantage of using a dummy trial-and-error firing circuit, which had pinpointed the precise area of the bandwidths the FBI had jammed. Mohsen had already switched to bandwidths beyond the range of the three-year-old technology the Feds had in the field—technology that wasn't military-grade, making it far easier to counter.

Behzad was taking more photos. "Did we have to take out the motorbike guys, Mohsen? They were just kids."

"Couldn't be helped."

Mohsen sensed Behzad's distaste for the dirty war they were engaged in, but he didn't share his brother's qualms about what he'd done. The cell could not be compromised. It was cold logic. Taking out the two young Iranian-Americans meant that the Feds couldn't interrogate them, find out who had recruited them in America and how. Even tenuous links to elements within the network could lead to the Feds joining up the dots of the disparate groups who were operating at large.

The importance of attention to detail, as well as the paramount importance of the mission, had been drilled into all of them.

Mohsen would kill his own brother if it enabled the death of the target—or ensured the cell wasn't compromised. Needs must. The end justifies the means.

He remembered the psychological tests he'd sat in Tehran. He had been given the scenario: *How would you feel if you had to kill your brother?* He had just smiled and said, "Whatever it takes." And that was that. His heart rate, he found out later, didn't spike at all when he said it. And that had impressed those higher up in Quds Force, the special forces unit of the Revolutionary Guards.

He didn't know if Behzad had done the same tests. But he assumed he wouldn't be on the mission if he too hadn't given a clear response.

The mission was king.

Mohsen reflected on how things were going. If he was honest, it was getting a bit messy. The plan had been simple: eliminate each of the Delta operatives, one at a time. But something had gone wrong, and it had brought the heat of the FBI on their tail. And that complicated things. He would much rather keep things simple. Simple was good.

The more he thought of the mission, the more focused he became. Blinkered, almost. He remembered the day his team was told about the assassinations, and the identities of those involved. He'd felt as if his heart had been ripped out by its roots.

For years he had nursed a similar hurt. Some nights, when he couldn't sleep, he thought about the bespectacled, brilliant scientist. His brother—the quietest boy in his school. Mohsen had always admired him. Protected him down the years. Stood up to bullies who had laughed at his bookishness.

Mohsen remembered the funeral. He remembered falling to his knees, crying unashamedly. But the years hadn't healed his pain. And now there was just emptiness in Mohsen's soul that couldn't be fixed.

The sound of Behzad groaning loudly snapped him out of his thoughts.

"The bomb technicians are well within range," his brother said.

"I'm not interested in them. This is about Vincenza." He trained his binoculars on the restaurant windows, spotting Meyerstein inside. "She's speaking to Vincenza now."

Behzad took more pictures. "Line of sight not perfect."

Mohsen stared at Vincenza. The man who had been part of the team that had killed his brother. Mohsen had said a silent prayer when he took on the mission—that he would not return until each and every member of the six-man American team had been wiped out.

"I don't like this Reznick guy running around," Behzad said. "He's going to be a problem."

"We'll deal with him in good time."

"What the hell are they talking about in there?"

"By all accounts, Vincenza is a stubborn son of a bitch. Pissed off every officer he ever encountered."

Behzad fired off more photos. "She's getting pretty animated with him."

Mohsen's earpiece buzzed. It had to be their handler.

"Yes, sir?" he said.

A deep breath. "The situation has been reappraised."

"Copy that."

"Code four two nine." It was the kill code to take out whoever was in their way, including Meyerstein.

Mohsen's heart skipped a beat. "Very good, sir."

"Do not let us down."

Mohsen stared through the binoculars at Meyerstein, and smiled.

Twenty-Seven

Meyerstein waited until Vincenza's girlfriend was escorted out of the rear of the restaurant. Then she pulled up a seat beside him. She caught a whiff of booze and cigarettes on his breath. His eyes were glazed.

"Here's how it's going to work, Mr. Vincenza. We're going to take you out of here, to a place of safety, just like Daisy."

"Do I look like the kind of guy who needs a babysitter?"

"Mr. Vincenza, I know all about you. I know about your role within Delta."

He said nothing.

"It was Jon Reznick who notified us about the bomb."

"Reznick? Bullshit."

Meyerstein shook her head. "He tracked you down to warn you of a threat. It's all about your mission in Tehran."

Vincenza knocked back his glass of red wine.

"Two guys on a motorbike. One gets off and clips a magnetic bomb onto the underside of your car. A matter of seconds, and they were off."

"Christ, you're serious . . ."

"Do you think this is a game? You have a choice. Either you exit the premises with my officers willingly, or we take you down here and now. The decision is yours."

"Where's Reznick now?" said Vincenza.

"Not far."

Meyerstein's cell phone rang.

"Martha," the Director's voice said. "O'Donoghue."

"Sir, I was about to call in with an update."

"What's Reznick saying about what happened? That was our best chance of a lead."

"Sir, I've not spoken to him. He's in transit to the command vehicle."

"He executed two American citizens, Martha. We've got a firestorm coming our way on this."

Meyerstein sighed as Vincenza got to his feet and began to pace the restaurant, muttering to himself.

"Sir," she said, "if you'll just let me—"

"Martha, he's crossed the line. He's blown the best lead we had. But I guess you know that already."

"Sir, I don't want to jump to conclusions until I know all the facts. Reznick was on this before anyone. He was the one who tracked down Vincenza."

"He's blown a chance to get vital intel. Do you know what Counterterrorism are saying?"

"Sir, I deal in real intel. And facts. Fact number one—we don't know what happened up there. Only Reznick does."

"I don't give a damn—"

Out of the corner of her eye, a razor-thin red beam shone through the window.

"Look out!" she shouted as a red dot locked on to Vincenza's head. Time seemed to slow down and then stop.

A bullet ripped through the windows, shattering the glass, flooring Vincenza. He lay prostrate in a pool of blood, as the shouting began and chaos ensued.

Meyerstein had been flung to the floor when the glass shattered. Her mind was racing as Stamper ran into the room. She looked up and pointed to a position high up in the hills. "Forty-five-degree angle it came in at," she said. "I want Malibu shut down. Nothing goes in or out. D'you hear me?"

Stamper nodded, then slipped on the bloody floor.

"I'm on it, Martha." He got to his feet and scrambled across the restaurant to the rear exit.

Meyerstein was hauled through a side door by her team and onto the Pacific Highway, back to the safety of the command center vehicle.

A young LA counterterrorism Fed was waiting. "Ma'am, we've got countless agents and police now scouring the houses overlooking the highway. Roadblocks set up in every direction."

Meyerstein's heart was racing. She looked out the window at the lights on the hill.

"What are we talking about?"

"Military sniper, I'd suggest."

"Reznick cautioned that they might be watching," she said.

"This is a targeted assassination. The bomb attached to Vincenza's car—it was pure chance that Reznick caught sight of that. But it didn't stop them. Like most pros, they had a backup plan. They didn't come all this way to miss their man, and they're not going to be satisfied until every member of the Delta team from Tehran is wiped out."

"Three are dead. We're trying to track down two. That leaves Reznick. He must be protected. These Iranians can't win."

The counterterrorism guy nodded, but said nothing.

"What's the latest on the two guys killed up in the canyon?"

"Update just came in. Just as Reznick said, they were taken out long-range, just like Vincenza. From half a mile, maybe more."

"Ballistics backs that up?"

"They will. First responders said it's clear it isn't 9mm slugs we're talking about. Shots darn near tore the kids' bodies apart."

"IDs on the two kids?"

"Americans."

"What else?"

"Parents were Iranian."

"What happened to them?"

"We're piecing it together. UCLA students—probably radicalized. The parents by all accounts didn't know a goddamn thing."

"What about their computers?"

"Early days. Forensics will comb laptops, cell phone records. We'll build up a picture."

Meyerstein slumped into a chair and spun it around to face the young Fed. "What a goddamn mess."

"Our problem is if this gets out . . ."

"The American people don't want to hear about some Iranian hit squad roaming around the country, taking out people in Florida, California, and God knows where."

The young man nodded.

"Why didn't they take out Reznick when they took care of the two Iranian-American students?" asked Meyerstein.

"My gut feeling? A separate cell was tasked with following the two young men to ensure they were taken care of if they got into trouble."

"So the triggerman might not have known that was Reznick on their tail?"

"Compartmentalize . . . need-to-know. You know the drill."

Meyerstein's mind flashed up images of the bullets ripping through the window and into Vincenza's body. She closed her eyes.

"What's the NSA saying?"

"They're tracing calls to both the students' cell phones, which we have. But the traces are bouncing around everywhere. Calls are encrypted and virtually unhackable. It'll take time."

"We should never underestimate the Iranians."

"One of the best special forces in the world. Technical skills and know-how built up over many years . . . They train Hezbollah, pass on most of their knowledge to them. Bombs, counterinsurgency, terrorism, intelligence—you name it."

Meyerstein sighed. "Shows what we're dealing with. They still got Vincenza and wiped out the two Iranian-Americans who were on their goddamn side. How is that possible?"

"They're resourceful, ruthless, and able to adjust plans in a fast-moving situation—the hallmarks of any special forces."

A hard knock at the door, and a SWAT team leader stepped into the command vehicle.

"Did you get Reznick?" Meyerstein asked him.

"We got Jon Reznick."

"Where is he?"

"At a secure facility."

"On whose goddamn orders?"

"The President's national security advisor."

Twenty-Eight

It was a high-speed, thirty-minute journey west along the Pacific Coast Highway to the Point Mugu naval air base.

Meyerstein sat throughout the journey in quiet contemplation. Events were getting out of control. There were going to be more deaths unless this cell was destroyed.

She felt the pressure building. O'Donoghue would be taking flak from the intelligence community. He wasn't averse to replacing a team and worrying about the consequences later.

A security guard escorted her deep into the bowels of the base, along with Roy Stamper and the SWAT team leader. Down shiny corridors, air-conditioning units growling low in the background. The guard was replaced by a naval detail as they moved into a secure area.

The lead naval officer said, "Ma'am, you're the only one with base clearance. They'll have to wait here."

Stamper and the SWAT team leader each took a seat, settling down to wait for her return. She moved on with the new escort to an elevator. Then up to a suite of offices on the top floor.

Captain Daniel Frostrop, the base commander, sat behind a desk in the large corner office. He wore a charcoal-gray suit, white shirt, and tightly knotted brown tie. He leaned back in his chair. "Take a seat, Meyerstein."

The naval officer escorting her shut the door, and Meyerstein sat down.

A moment later there was a knock, and a tall middle-aged man wearing a dark suit entered the room. Frostrop got up from his seat. "Brigadier General Andrew T. Belmont, Homeland Security, a counterterrorism expert and advisor to the President on national security issues. This is FBI Assistant Director Martha Meyerstein."

Meyerstein nodded but said nothing as Belmont took a seat at the back of the room.

Frostrop sat down again. "You're probably wondering why we have Reznick here."

"I'd be interested in your explanation," said Meyerstein.

Frostrop grimaced. "You see . . . I was just speaking to General Belmont, and we both agree that this is the best place for Reznick until further notice."

Meyerstein shifted in her seat. "Under whose authority?"

Frostrop nodded in the direction of Belmont. The brigadier general held up a letter showing the presidential seal. "This gives me carte blanche to decide what we do with Reznick."

"Do you know anything about Jon Reznick?"

"I'm well aware of his record," Belmont said. "And I'm well aware that he is now used by the FBI on a freelance basis."

Meyerstein said nothing.

"Look, Meyerstein, just to clarify—I'm not here to cause you problems. Or the FBI. The Bureau is the lead agency. But Jon Reznick . . . he's my concern."

"He's also my concern," she replied.

"And I respect that."

Meyerstein studied Belmont's clean-cut features. She thought there was a coldness around his eyes.

"Has anyone interviewed him?"

Belmont shook his head. "Not yet. We only know what the SWAT guys relayed to us."

"Which was?"

"Sniper downed the two young would-be bombers."

"And what does that tell you?"

"We've got a problem, that's what it tells me."

"What else do I need to know?" said Meyerstein.

Belmont cleared his throat. "Within the last few minutes, shortly before you arrived, we got news on Albert Rain, another Delta operator."

"And?"

"And it's not good. Rain's body has been found, washed up on a remote shore of Lake Champlain, near Burlington, Vermont."

Meyerstein took a long hard look at Belmont.

"That's why we're keeping Reznick out of sight," he said. "We can't take any more chances."

"You want my take on this?"

Belmont shrugged. "Sure, go right ahead."

"They'll only be after one thing."

"Reznick."

"Precisely," said Meyerstein.

"And that's why we've brought him here. No one needs to know a thing."

"There's a flaw in that logic, General."

Belmont frowned. "And what precisely is that?"

"They'll check the nearest secure facilities. The nearest military bases."

Belmont ran a hand through his short hair. "Do you think they've got the capabilities to penetrate this base's security?"

"I wouldn't put anything past the Quds Force."

"You can't be serious . . . I mean, for Iran to contemplate such a move it would be near-suicide. We operate in the shadows. Those are the rules."

Meyerstein got up from her chair and paced the room. "They've picked off four of these ex–Delta operators, one at a time. It wouldn't make sense to leave any alive. They've been instructed to find them and kill them all. Simple."

Frostrop spoke up. "This is an easy decision, Meyerstein. Reznick can hide out here until the coast is clear."

"You're not listening. Besides, what if he doesn't want to?"

Frostrop sighed. "What do you mean?"

"I mean, do you think Reznick, from what we know about him, is the type of guy who's content to just hide out? Do you?"

Frostrop said nothing, and Belmont shrugged.

"I know Reznick quite well," Meyerstein said. "I think you've overlooked a way to deal with this."

Belmont scratched the tip of his nose. "What way?"

"There are risks involved, I have to warn you."

"I don't like risks."

Meyerstein smiled. "Depends what sort of hand you're dealt."

"What are you proposing?"

"I want to speak to Reznick," said Meyerstein. "Face to face. Now."

Belmont examined his hands, pressing back the cuticles on his fingernails.

"Why?"

"I want to see if we can use him to get closer to them."

⌣

Brigadier General Belmont accompanied Meyerstein deep into the restricted area of the base. They headed down a series of corridors until they reached a basement tunnel that led to a separate building.

She felt disorientated as they approached a screened-off area, armed guards blocking the entrance.

IDs were checked and they were buzzed through. She peered through a small window into what looked like an interview room, with one table, two chairs, and a handcuffed Jon Reznick pacing the room. Two cameras were placed high up on the walls.

Meyerstein turned to Belmont. "I need to speak to him alone."

Belmont shook his head. "No."

"I do this on my own, or forget it. And I want the handcuffs off."

"Why?"

"He's no threat to me."

A long pause. "Very well," said Belmont, "but I'll be watching through the window."

Belmont handed Meyerstein the keys for the cuffs. She entered the room, the door locking automatically behind her.

"How are you?" she said.

Reznick glanced up at one of the cameras and shook his head. He turned to face her. "You mind explaining what the hell I'm doing in this shithole?"

"It's just temporary."

He stared at her. "You mind uncuffing me?"

Meyerstein stepped forward and uncuffed him. They were standing so close that she could feel the warmth of his breath.

Reznick stood in silence, searching her face for answers.

Meyerstein took a step back. "This is payback, Tehran-style."

"If you dish it out, you've got to be able to take it."

"Pity you can't share that sentiment with Tiny, Dorfman, Vincenza, and Rain."

"What do you mean?"

"They took out Vincenza at the restaurant. Long-range. Just been told Rain's body was washed up at Lake Champlain, Vermont. I'm sorry."

Reznick sat down in a chair, silent. Face as impassive as ever. Eyes clear, almost unfathomable.

"What was Albert like?" she asked.

"Albert was the quietest of the crew. Content to just be there. Dorfman was the one doing the wisecracking." He shook his head. "I remember Albert showed me a picture of his newborn daughter that his wife had emailed him, when we were taking cover in an informant's house in Falluja."

Meyerstein felt her throat tighten.

"The pride in his eyes was something any father would understand. He didn't tell anyone else, only me. I sometimes wondered why that was. Maybe it was because the rest of the guys pulled his leg about him being a cracker, having grown up in the backwoods of Georgia. *Ain't she something, Jon?* he would say."

Meyerstein let out a long sigh.

"Tell me more about how they got Blaine," he said.

"Vincenza was gunned down as I spoke to him at Nobu."

Reznick stared at her for what seemed like an eternity.

"You were right," she said. "They were watching us, Jon."

He bowed his head. "What about the two who planted the bomb?"

"Jon, you must have inadvertently got in between the two students on the bike and the shadow."

"Yup."

"Where was the triggerman shooting from?"

"No idea. Too far from me."

Meyerstein paced the room for a few moments. "I've got a proposition for you, Jon. I need your help."

"First get me out of this place."

"Jon, that might be a problem, but there's someone here who can make that problem go away." Meyerstein stared at the mirror, through which she knew Belmont was watching, and signaled for him to join them.

"Listen," said Reznick, "I don't want to hear some horseshit story about *we can't do this and we can't do that.* They've just killed my Delta buddies. And I'm not going to sit here with my thumb up my ass."

"Jon, listen to me. You need to realize—"

"Get me out of here or—"

Just then, Belmont entered the room.

"Who the fuck are you?" said Reznick.

"I advise on national security matters. My name's Belmont."

Reznick stared at him in silence.

"This is complicated, Jon. The Iranians want to take you out. But we're not going to allow it."

"I want to see if we can't come to some sort of arrangement," interjected Meyerstein.

"You talking about a deal?" said Reznick.

Meyerstein pointed to the door. "You want out of here?"

He nodded.

"There are risks involved in taking you out of here. Risks for all of us. Do we all agree that we want to track down these sons of bitches?"

Reznick and Belmont both nodded.

"Jon, what if I said that I want to use you?"

"In what way?"

"As bait for the Iranians."

"You want me to lure them? I'm the honey, right?"

"I wouldn't put it quite like that," she said.

"I'll do it. On one condition . . ."

Meyerstein's cell phone rang, interrupting the conversation. "Goddamn," she said, reaching into her jacket pocket. She didn't recognize the number.

"Meyerstein."

There was a silence. Then someone spoke.

"You really need to get new encryption for your phone, Assistant Director."

A male voice. She didn't recognize it.

Meyerstein froze for a second. "Who's this?"

"Don't play games. You Americans are very fond of games. Well—guess what?—so am I."

"I think you've got the wrong number," said Meyerstein.

"Oh, we've got the right number, Assistant Director Martha Meyerstein of the Federal Bureau of Investigation."

"What the hell do you want?"

"We want Reznick."

Meyerstein's heart skipped a beat.

"In thirty minutes, we'll call you back on this number. We will have more details of how this is going to work."

Twenty-Nine

The specter of the growing threat galvanized Meyerstein. Sitting alongside Belmont in a secure conference room, she hooked up an emergency videoconference with the National Security Council in Washington, as they tried to get a handle on what and who they were dealing with. She scribbled down notes as the faces of the President's most senior military and intelligence advisors stared down from the large screens.

Meyerstein listened as arguments raged back and forth among the experts. She ordered her thoughts and plan of action before she made her first input.

"I'd like to know what's the latest from the NSA on tracking this call."

Mitch Chivers, an NSA senior analyst, said, "Ma'am, this should be easy for us, but in this case, it's not."

"What do you mean?"

Chivers glanced at his laptop. "I'm just checking the latest from my team as we speak. We believe the call originated in California—specifically the Santa Monica area. We just can't narrow it down any further. They must be using more advanced encryption. But we're still working on it."

"Not good enough. Are you telling me the NSA can't crack this?"

Counterterrorism expert Ronald McMaster put up his hand. "If I can jump in here, Martha. My best analysts have been working on this, but I'm afraid, at this early stage, we don't yet have verifiable intel—"

"Jesus! What *do* we know?"

"We are certain these are Iranian Quds Force operatives. And they seem prepared to up the ante. Tehran knows the ramifications if they conduct any terrorist acts on our soil."

"I want names, and the modus operandi of this cell," said Meyerstein. "Is that clear?"

McMaster leaned forward and tapped a few keys on his laptop. Simultaneously, images of five Quds Force operatives appeared on the middle screen.

"We believe these are our guys. Still checking the voice analysis. The guy in the middle is the leader, Mohsen Sazegara. He's here to avenge the death of his brother."

"His brother?"

"Ali Sazegara, a nuclear-fusion scientist who was blown up in Tehran six years ago."

Meyerstein leaned back in her seat. "So it's personal . . ." She turned and looked at Belmont. "You wanna jump in, General?"

Belmont sighed. "It is personal, Martha. Ali Sazegara was killed just yards from his home in a Tehran suburb. Reznick led that part of the mission. He was the triggerman."

Meyerstein stood up. "And when the hell were you going to tell me about Sazegara, and how his brother was taken out by Reznick and his Delta crew?"

Belmont cleared his throat. "It's always on a need-to-know basis. That's just the way it is."

"Bullshit. You put my team and me at risk. Not to mention Reznick and his Delta crew."

"You need to get the right perspective on this, Martha."

Meyerstein ignored Belmont, and sat back down.

"Ronald, do you think taking out Reznick is the most important hit?"

"Yeah," said McMaster. "All that Shiite, blood brother stuff. It's personal and it's bad for Reznick."

Meyerstein looked at her watch. "Fifteen minutes until they call back. How do we get on the front foot?"

McMaster said, "I think we should get Reznick out of here. Take him to the other side of the country."

"You clearly don't know Jon Reznick," said Meyerstein. "He will not want to hide from these guys."

"What else do you propose?"

"We don't know what their next move is going to be. It's not the usual Iranian modus operandi to want to enter into discussions."

"I've got to agree with you on this," said McMaster. "I fear there may be something bigger here."

"Something else to consider," Meyerstein said. "Do you think these guys in California have gone rogue?"

McMaster winced. "It's a long shot . . ."

"Think about it. What if the brother of this dead nuclear scientist is ripping up the rule book and following his own agenda—to hell with the consequences?"

"From everything we know about Quds, this is not how they play the game. They're usually tight. Very, very disciplined."

Meyerstein took a few moments to reply. "What if we're wrong? What if these guys have stepped off the deep end? What if they're not planning to go back to Tehran until all the Delta guys are dead?"

No one said a word.

Meyerstein headed back to the interview room, where Reznick was leaning against a wall, arms folded. She faced him, hands on hips, and outlined what she knew as he listened intently.

"What do you reckon's going on here, Jon?"

"With regards to?"

"With regards to why they're going to call back. Any minute now."

Reznick stared at her. "They're fucking with us, that's what they're doing."

Meyerstein sighed. "Is that your considered analysis?"

"Pretty much. We're all waiting on them to make the next move. But I guarantee you they've already made it."

"What do you mean?"

"They're playing you, they're playing me. They're playing all of us. My gut is telling me these guys are doing their own thing."

"What if I told you that one of the Iranians . . . that you killed his brother in Tehran."

Reznick said nothing.

"So where does that leave us?"

"They're going to try and kill me. No matter the cost. And make no mistake, revenge is everything to these guys."

"Jon, I—"

The shrill ringtone of Meyerstein's cell interrupted their conversation. She saw that the caller ID on her phone was changing, someone clearly scrambling the lines to avoid detection.

Meyerstein felt her heart rate quicken before she answered.

"Meyerstein."

A long sigh. "Good to speak to you again, Assistant Director."

"Thank you for calling back."

"I can hear the uncertainty in your voice, Meyerstein. It betrays your true feelings. I don't want to hurt you. As long as I get what I want."

Meyerstein closed her eyes. "What *do* you want?"

The man began to laugh.

"What the hell is so funny?"

"You know exactly what I want. Jon Reznick."

Meyerstein looked across at Reznick, who was staring back at her. Eyes cold, face inscrutable.

"No deal. Do you think the FBI would just hand over Reznick?'

"That is your final answer?"

"Yes, it is."

"Then, sadly, we're going to have to kill some innocent Americans, aren't we?" the man said.

The line went dead.

Thirty

The morning sun was streaming across the Hollywood Hills. Jerry Morlach was soaking up the rays, listening to an old Miles Davis album on his terrace, when his cell phone rang.

"I'm looking to speak to Jerry Franklin Morlach," an unfamiliar male voice said.

Morlach was immediately put on alert. He didn't know anyone who used his full name. The fact that this man had used it told him everything he had to know.

"I think you have the wrong number."

A long pause. "I'm a contract worker."

Morlach took a few moments to compose himself. He had been expecting the call. The two-tier code—his full name and the words *contract worker*—had been activated. The caller was from the CIA, who used Morlach as a back channel to Tehran, as and when required. But it had been years since he'd heard from Langley.

"I'm sorry, this is a bad line. It sounded like you said you're a contract worker."

"Yes, I am."

"What can I do for you?"

"Mr. Morlach, you may know my predecessor. His name was Stadler."

Morlach did indeed know who Stadler was. He wondered if the caller was a replacement.

"There are things we need to discuss. We want to talk. Frankly."

"Why?"

The man sighed. "You're the back channel for this deal, right?"

Morlach lit up a cigarette, sucking the smoke deep into his lungs. "I need to know that you are indeed who you claim you are."

"You need to make a call. They'll verify."

Morlach said nothing as he exhaled the smoke.

"The verification code is eight characters long. Do you have a pen handy?"

Morlach had a flawless memory for figures and didn't need a pen.

"I'm listening."

"Verification code is as follows: nine four four nine eight one, Delta, Delta. I'll call you back in an hour."

The line went dead.

Morlach pulled up the contact he had saved in his phone. Four rings, and a woman's voice: "Please give the verification code."

Morlach recited it. There was a long pause.

"I can confirm our contract worker has been deployed," the woman said.

"Thank you." He ended the call and waited. Exactly an hour after the first call, Morlach's cell rang.

He answered after one ring.

"We OK?" the man said.

"We're good."

"We have work to do."

"I'm listening."

"We are quite prepared to give Iran what they want."

Morlach said nothing.

"I mean, of course, Jon Reznick."

Morlach's stomach knotted at the mere mention of Reznick's name. "How do I know that what you say is true?"

"I think it's important we keep this channel of communication open at this time."

"You haven't answered my question."

"Which was?"

"How do I know that what you say is true?"

"You've got to trust me on this. The authorization for this move came from the top."

"So you want me to pass on this message?"

"That's precisely what I'm saying. I'll be back in touch."

Thirty-One

Meyerstein was running on adrenaline.

She endured another grueling videoconference call, this time with the Pentagon. NSA analysts checked and cross-referenced leads on the whereabouts of the caller they believed was in the Santa Monica area. But they couldn't pin down the location.

Meyerstein felt frustrated and apprehensive. She'd had too much coffee for her own good, her nerves shredded.

She picked up her cell and dialed her home number in Washington.

"Martha," her mother said, "you OK, honey?"

"Hi. Yes, I'm fine. Just got a couple of minutes. Checking in to see how the kids are."

"Just perfect. They miss you, obviously. Always asking when you'll be home."

Meyerstein closed her eyes. She felt bad. She always did when her work took her away from her family. But she knew the demands of the job. It was no nine-to-five.

"I've got a bit of a situation at work just now. So I haven't got long to talk to them. You mind putting them on?"

"I'm sorry, honey, but they're at after-school clubs. Piano and soccer."

"Damn. I'm working on Pacific Time. Sorry."

"You're in California?"

Meyerstein blew out her cheeks. "Yeah . . . Goddamn, I don't even know what time of day it is."

"Martha, I know . . . it isn't easy, honey. Your father was away a lot when you were growing up, too. Do you know what he used to say when I said how much you were missing him?"

"What was that?"

"He'd say, *She knows I love her. She knows I care for her. And I will always provide for her, despite being away from home most of the time.* He was always good at being rational."

Meyerstein sighed. "It's tough, it really is."

"I know. But you're tough. Look, the kids are great. And I'm only too delighted to look after them. Who better, right?"

"Thanks, Mom, appreciate that."

"Now, don't be worrying so much. They're safe and well. And in good health, thank God."

"Tell them I called. And that I love them. And kiss them good-night, will you?"

"Each and every night."

"Mom—love you."

Meyerstein had never felt so conflicted. Even when she was home, she struggled to stay interested in what her kids were up to, as she was always exhausted after work.

The more she thought about it, the more she worried she was becoming adrift from her family. The job was doing that to her. Day by day, month by month, year by year. It was eating away at her from within. She wondered if it was time to reassess her priorities.

"Meyerstein, videoconference room!" she heard Belmont shout.

Meyerstein switched straight back into work mode as she headed back to the videoconference facility. A huge screen was showing the FBI's National Counterterrorism Center in McLean.

"Gentlemen," she said, "any developments?"

Ronald McMaster punched a few keys on his laptop. A grainy photo was displayed of a man with light-brown skin, cell phone pressed to his ear.

"Got a breakthrough, ma'am. This is the latest shot we have of Mohsen Sazegara."

"Where and when was this taken?"

Counterterrorism specialist Mac Jackson put up his hand. "Hi, Martha. Yeah, this was taken seventy-two minutes ago at a Laundromat in Santa Monica."

"How are we only getting this now?"

"Long story. Face-recognition matches throwing up other IDs, but we're satisfied this is one of our guys. But here's the kicker—he doesn't live or work in Iran."

"You've gotta be kidding me."

"The face recognition matches a naturalized American citizen with dual Iranian citizenship. He lives in Corpus Christi, Texas. New identity."

"Shit."

"Indeed."

"What does he do?"

A long sigh, but no answer.

"I said what does he do?"

McMaster cleared his throat. "He's an engineer at defense contractor Methvens and Fischer."

"No, that can't be right. Jesus!"

Meyerstein stared up at the faces on the screens. "OK, let's focus here. How many times has he visited Tehran?"

"He's made seven return trips to see his brother-in-law in Hamadan in the last five years."

"Tell me about Mohsen Sazegara."

"He's not married. Fitness fanatic. Thirty-five. Black belt in karate. Member of three gun clubs in Texas. Very well-integrated and Westernized. And he's operating under the name Mozen. M-O-Z-E-N," he said, spelling it out.

"Have his details been circulated?"

"Intelligence and Homeland Security now have them."

"The cops?"

"Restricted to senior levels in Southern California."

Meyerstein nodded. She knew that if there was any leak from a sheriff or cop, the whole thing would turn into a media frenzy.

"What about his home in Corpus Christi?"

"Already combing through it. Forensics are searching his laptop, but nothing so far. Pretty advanced encryption by all accounts."

"Who's pulling the strings—local or foreign?"

"Maybe both. But we've run this around and we think this guy is leading the team."

"Guys, we're chasing shadows. What's their next move?"

"Martha, I don't think we can—"

"I said what's their next goddamn move?"

A brief pause. "The near-unanimous consensus is that a long-range sniper will pick off the next target, especially after Vincenza was gunned down long range and the two Iranian-American students were taken out the same way."

Meyerstein's mind was racing. She didn't know if it was too much coffee or too little sleep. Maybe both.

"How have we missed this guy?"

"The same way we missed the Boston bombers," said McMaster.

"That's not strictly true. We didn't miss those guys. We had a heads-up from the Russians."

McMaster and the rest of the guys up on-screen nodded.

"This is different," she said. "This guy should have been on our radar. He's not working on his own. What about the rest of his crew?"

A long silence opened up.

"You're keeping something from me. What the hell is it?"

McMaster rubbed his eyes. "Martha—Mohsen Sazegara was, at one time, on our radar."

"What?"

"The FBI had him under surveillance two years ago."

"So why did it end?"

"There were competing threats. We had to think triage . . . what was the most severe and urgent threat, then work back from there."

Meyerstein leaned back in her seat. "So the guy leading a cell that hunted down and killed ex–Delta operatives was once under our goddamn noses? Tell me you're joking."

"Sadly not."

"Who made that call?"

"Martha, I don't think it does anyone any good to trawl over—"

"Goddammit, who made that call?"

McMaster looked around at the faces at his end, before he turned to look at Meyerstein. "Authorization shows that it came from the San Antonio FBI field office."

"Who's in charge there?"

"Martha, I don't think blaming someone—"

"This is nothing to do with blaming someone. This is holding people accountable. Because if we don't, we're going to make these same mistakes over and over again. Who's in charge?"

"Special Agent in Charge is Charles Patterson."

"I need to speak to him, right now," said Meyerstein.

"The SAC is indisposed, Martha."

"What do you mean?"

"He's on honeymoon."

"I don't give a damn where he is. I need to know the rationale."

"Martha, it was the wrong call."

"Get me his number."

Mac gave her Patterson's number and Meyerstein abruptly ended the videoconference. Three rings and the call was picked up.

"This better be good," a man's voice rasped.

Meyerstein cleared her throat. "Charles, apologies for bothering you. Assistant Director Martha Meyerstein here."

"Is this a joke? Do you know what time it is?"

"This is no joke. We've got an emergency, Charles."

"What kind of emergency?"

"A guy the San Antonio field office had under surveillance. Look, is this a secure line you're on?"

"Yeah. Who are we talking about?"

Meyerstein rubbed her shoulders to relieve her tense muscles. "Mohsen Sazegara. Dual citizenship—Iranian-American. Worked for a defense contractor. Under surveillance."

"I know the one you mean. But what do you mean we had him under surveillance?"

"I mean you lifted the surveillance on him."

"I did no such thing."

Meyerstein was momentarily thrown by his answer. She quickly scrolled through the email McMaster had just sent through. "I'm sorry, I have a copy of the instruction you sent out on the seventh of March this year."

"Listen, Meyerstein, I sent no such thing."

"I have it in front of me, with your signature."

"Not mine. There is no goddamn way I authorized that."

Meyerstein wondered if the SAC was just not willing to take the flak. "Are you positive? I'm going to be double-checking this."

"One hundred percent. I did not authorize that. You say the document has my signature? Has that been verified? Because I think you'll find that signature isn't mine."

Meyerstein closed her eyes for a moment and sighed. She hadn't seen this coming.

"Listen," he said, "get the handwriting guys at Forensic Document Examination to check the signature. It ain't mine."

Meyerstein thought he sounded genuine. "Charles, we'll check this out. You might be hearing from Counterterrorism. Probably want to keep your cell charged."

"What the hell is going on, Martha?"

"I need to go, Charles. Enjoy the rest of your honeymoon."

Meyerstein ended the call and hooked up again with McLean. She relayed the information to Jackson and the rest of the counterterrorism specialists around the table.

"That's impossible," Jackson said.

"Except it's not. I want the best FBI forensic handwriting expert to check over this instruction from Charles. He's adamant it wasn't him, and I believe him."

"Copy that. We're on it. This will take a couple of hours, Martha. I'd suggest you get some rest. Grab it while you can."

Meyerstein was about to protest, but she knew it made sense. She realized she hadn't slept in the last twenty-four hours. She ended the videoconference and was shown to a suite.

Three hours later, a gentle knocking on the door woke Meyerstein. It took her a few moments to get her bearings. "I'll be there in ten minutes," she shouted.

She jumped out of bed and quickly freshened up with a hot shower. She touched up her makeup, got dressed, popped a mint in her mouth, and returned to the videoconference room.

The face of handwriting specialist Morton Greenbank was up on one of the screens. "Ma'am, Special Agent Greenbank. I can see how they did this."

"Did what?"

"The signature is not Patterson's."

"What do you mean?"

"It looks like Patterson's at first glance. But it's not. They hacked the FBI."

Meyerstein shook her head. "This is getting worse. How could they have done this?"

"We're still trying to figure that out. But I can confirm there has been a clear breach down in San Antonio. Someone accessed a server and got to work."

"FBI cybersecurity has been breached? Are you kidding me?"

"Sadly not, ma'am. It's a constant battle to stay ahead of the hackers and countries looking to exploit our vulnerabilities. They do this all the time."

"Yeah, but how?"

"Any weak spot or local weak spot might have provided the opportunity. Perhaps a memory stick that was swapped, infecting a local computer down there, allowing them access. Break into an agent's car, and any laptop or flash drive in there could be their way in. It's low-tech, but very effective."

"OK, how long till you determine exactly how this happened?"

"I'll have it within an hour."

"Can you also determine how this false signature got onto the document and into our system?"

"I'll get to it."

Greenbank's face disappeared, replaced by McMaster. The adjacent screen flashed up a picture of a thickset man with pale brown skin and piercing black eyes.

"Martha, we've got a critical update."

"Who's this?"

"This is Mohsen's brother Behzad. He lives in Dallas, organizes tours for wealthy Texans to Middle Eastern tourist haunts. Jordan, Egypt, and so on. His wife and three kids took a flight to Tehran ten days ago. He's disappeared."

"What else do we know about this guy?"

"Westernized, like his brother. Never been under FBI surveillance."

"What else?"

"Here's the kicker. He bought ammonium nitrate at a Home Depot in Austin last month."

Meyerstein put her head in her hands. "And he and his brother are here in Southern California."

"Martha, this is a fast-moving situation. We have hundreds of officers and agents doing stop-and-searches of vehicles and individuals across Santa Monica. We're also going door-to-door on the houses overlooking Nobu in Malibu. Still nothing."

"Are you telling me there's no surveillance footage from someone's front yard or driveway?"

"Martha, each and every house is being checked over. It takes time."

"We haven't got time."

"I'm well aware of that."

Meyerstein's phone rang. The caller ID was a number she didn't recognize. Before she answered, she looked up at the screen. "Are we doing a trace on my cell?"

McMaster nodded. "Already in place. Go right ahead."

Meyerstein answered the call. "Yes?"

"We don't want to hurt anyone." The man's voice again. "Really, we don't. So you're going to give us Reznick. Hand him over."

Meyerstein felt her blood turn cold. "Listen, we don't do deals."

"Don't you?"

"Not with you. Not with anyone."

A long sigh. "And that's your final word?"

Meyerstein looked up at the screen. McMaster was nodding. "We want dialogue."

"You're trying my patience, Meyerstein."

Meyerstein felt her stomach knot. "We don't do deals."

"Then I'm afraid Americans will die. And it will be on your head, Meyerstein."

Thirty-Two

Mohsen Sazegara parked the car on the third level of the parking garage in downtown Santa Monica. He glanced in the rearview mirror and made sure there wasn't anyone else around. Satisfied there was no one to disturb him, he got out and popped the trunk.

Inside was a backpack. He took it out and slung it over his shoulder, slamming the trunk hard. Then he locked the car, took the stairs down, and walked across 2nd Street to the four-screen Laemmle cinema.

They were showing a number of European arthouse films. He asked for a ticket to a gloomy-sounding Scandinavian movie and handed over a twenty-dollar bill. Taking his change, he headed into the auditorium, which was nearly full—maybe around forty people.

Mohsen sat in the middle of the front row and placed his backpack under the seat, tight between his feet. He took off his shades and stared up at the screen. The film was about a loner detective investigating the death of a politician's mistress.

He heard whispered voices several rows behind him.

"*I wish he would get his goddamn head out of the way . . .*"

"*Why is he sitting in the front row . . . ?*"

Sazegara afforded himself a wry smile in the darkness.

If only they knew, he thought.

He stared at the dank images of a Copenhagen alley, as these cinemagoers in far-off California absorbed the film's message. The Western liberal mindset at work. A "progressive" society, on the surface.

He had seen it as he integrated into the Texan life. Kids who didn't respect their parents, a lack of discipline in poorly run schools, and the consumer-driven quest for a new car, new gun, new house—and, invariably, a new wife.

The rustling of candy wrappers a few rows behind him brought him back to his surroundings. The Danish voices on the screen boomed out of the surround-sound speakers.

As he thought about what he was going to do, his mind was on fire. It was like he was about to be consumed by a euphoric madness.

The sense of expectation grew within him, making him so giddy he nearly burst out laughing.

He closed his eyes for a few moments. *Discipline. You must be disciplined.* He could hear his handler's voice now. The calm, authoritative tone. In his mind's eye, he saw his mother again. The terrible anguish contorting her face as she buried her son—Mohsen's brother, the brilliant nuclear scientist.

The helplessness he'd seen in her eyes consumed and drove him. He had no remorse at the best of times. And now? He felt nothing. And that was good.

He was afraid of nothing. Of no one.

Mohsen opened his eyes and felt cleansed. Refreshed. He took another few moments to compose himself. Then he bent over and undid his backpack, feeling the paper McDonald's bag. Inside the bag was the cold metal of the aerosol container. The silent killer.

He placed the paper bag carefully underneath his seat.

The device was primed. It would fill the air with a deadly chemical, synthesized in a basement lab in a Houston suburb by one of his crew. An opium-like derivative of fentanyl—carfentanil, one of the drugs used by the Russian Special Forces in the Moscow theater siege. Ten thousand times more powerful than morphine.

Mohsen contemplated the sequence of events about to unfold. Within the container was the cell phone receiver. A text message sent to the number would activate the device and release the killer chemical.

Confusion would reign for a few moments. He imagined people screaming as they gasped for breath. Then they would die. A painful, bewildering death.

Mohsen leaned over and picked up the empty backpack. Then he walked out of the cinema and back across the street. He took the stairs two at a time, and got back into his car.

Mohsen took a few deep breaths before pulling away. After leaving the garage, he drove through Santa Monica for a mile, eventually parking in a quiet street off the Pacific Coast Highway. The sky was red.

He took out his cell phone. He texted the number, and closed his eyes.

Thirty-Three

"Oh shit, this is really happening," Meyerstein said. She felt sick as she stared up at the footage from the hazmat team inside the cinema. Twisted bodies lay between and across the seats, some with their tongues protruding as if gasping for air, some with eyes wide. A few had made it as far as the exit doors, but had breathed in too much of the gas to survive.

She turned and looked at Belmont. "Forty-three dead. I can't bear to think about it."

Belmont said nothing.

The voice of the caller lingered long in her mind. *Then I'm afraid Americans will die. And it will be on your head, Meyerstein.*

Those were his last words. Her decision had cost dozens of lives. She was to blame. Why the hell hadn't she tried to play along more? She should have played for time.

Shit.

She tried to push the negative and corrosive thoughts to one side, as the largest screen in the videoconference room switched to the FBI's Counterterrorism Center in McLean.

"Martha," said FBI Special Agent John Veitch, "we got the latest assessment."

"Shoot."

"This is a four-man crew. All Iranian-Americans."

"Mohsen Sazegara?"

An image appeared on a third screen. It was from a surveillance camera in a parking garage in Santa Monica. It showed a tall, muscular man with a backpack slung over his shoulder.

"This is him," said Veitch. "Cool as a fucking cucumber. This guy walked into the cinema and watched a film for fifteen minutes—no more—and then left the device, primed. He triggered it by remote control from a cell phone."

Meyerstein took a few moments to digest the facts. She knew the importance of viewing evidence and information dispassionately. She had to fight against this turning personal.

"This is not Iran's usual modus operandi when it comes to the West," she said.

"They've crossed a line. They know the rules. It points to Sazegara and his crew going rogue."

"He must know that we'll wipe them out."

Veitch shrugged. "Maybe that's what he wants . . . A head-to-head confrontation. Revenge for his brother."

Meyerstein sighed. "Where is Sazegara now?"

"After leaving the cinema and returning to the garage, we tracked the vehicle to a parking lot on the eastern outskirts of Santa Monica. Here's the footage right now."

A few moments later, Meyerstein watched as Sazegara pulled up in the parking lot, got out his vehicle, and headed for the stairwell, backpack over his shoulder. Then the screen froze.

"What happened?" she asked.

"Jamming technology. Blocked all the surveillance cameras within a one-hundred-yard radius. Likely he drove away in another vehicle, or was driven away."

Meyerstein shook her head. She thought about what Reznick had said.

"They're fucking with us."

"Big time," said Veitch. "The President is meeting his closest advisors as we speak, including O'Donoghue. They're assessing all options. Including . . ."

"Including what?"

"Martha, they might cut Reznick loose."

Meyerstein wondered if she had heard right. "Tell me you're joking?"

"Martha, I don't like it any more than you do. But we have to look at the big picture."

"Are we just going to hand Reznick over to them? The United States of America is serious about this? Have I missed something?"

"It's one of the options on the table."

Meyerstein got to her feet and paced the room, all eyes from the screen on her. "One of the options on the table? One of the god-damn options on the table? Are you guys serious? Well, you know what, it's bullshit."

"Martha, I know this is personal for you," said Veitch. "You brought Reznick onto a couple of operations. But you need to see the way the wind is blowing on this one."

"Go to hell. This isn't personal. What about the forty-three inno-cent Americans just murdered by this maniac? If we capitulate to their demands, this won't be the end of it. I will not hand anyone over."

"No matter the cost?"

Meyerstein's heart rate was up a notch. "We don't play by their rules."

"Martha, the fallout from this could be immense."

"It already is. No way do we bend to them. How the hell can we guarantee that these guys are just going to melt away? This is a suicide mission for them. They know they can't go back to their regular lives, or escape to Tehran."

"I think all they want is Reznick," said Veitch.

"I don't give a damn what they want. We will hunt them down. And we will sort this out our way."

"No matter the consequences?"

"The consequences are already too damaging."

"I'm not disagreeing, Martha. But sometimes you've got to make deals. It's the name of the game."

"I can't believe what I'm hearing."

"I'm sorry."

"So am I."

Meyerstein sat back down. She wondered how this was going to play out.

Her cell vibrated in her jacket pocket. Another number she didn't know. Her stomach knotted.

"Meyerstein," she said into her phone.

Silence. But she sensed it was *him*.

Meyerstein signaled to those on the videoconference screen, who were tracing her call. One of the Feds nodded in reply.

"Meyerstein," she said. "Who's this?"

"Your voice sounds strained," the familiar voice said.

Meyerstein cleared her throat. "I'm—"

"Yes, there's definitely tension in your voice. I'm not surprised. Are you shocked?"

Meyerstein was tempted to curse him. But she remained calm. She closed her eyes and prayed that the NSA would somehow track the call, despite knowing it was almost certainly being bounced off every cell phone tower possible in order to mask the GPS location. She glanced at her iPad. Messages were coming in from the NSA, trying to pinpoint the location: *Vermont, Canada, Florida, California, Germany* . . . The list of false trails mounted up.

"If you're wondering, you'll never trace me."

Meyerstein said nothing.

"Cat got your tongue, Assistant Director?" The voice dripped with sarcasm.

Meyerstein sighed.

"How does it feel to have someone walk into your country and do some wetwork?"

"What do you want?"

"You might not believe me, but I didn't want to kill those people."

"But you did."

"Yes, I did. And sadly, it's going to happen again. And again, until we get what we want."

"I think you must understand there are some lines in the sand that we don't cross."

"Lines in the sand get redrawn all the time, don't they?"

Meyerstein closed her eyes.

"America is very good at drawing lines in the sand," the voice said. "And lines on a map."

"I need more time."

"You're out of time. We're already at our next destination."

"Goddammit!"

"I think you're starting to understand how serious we are. We're making progress."

"Give me some time."

"I'll call back in precisely one hour's time. And then we will talk about handing over Mr. Reznick."

Thirty-Four

"Martha, the NSA have got a fix on the phone!" Veitch said.

Meyerstein felt her heart rate hike up a notch. "Location?"

"Ten minutes. Oxnard, right on the beach."

"Let's do this."

Meyerstein headed outside to a waiting SUV, accompanied by three LA Feds, before being driven off the base at high speed. The radio crackled into life, speakers on.

"Be advised," Veitch said, "there's a SWAT team on the outskirts of Oxnard. One minute from the location."

"Have we got more details?"

"Twelve sixty-two Santa Cruz Avenue. Colonial-style house, stairs up to the door on the first level. Double garage. Owner of the house is Jackson Melrose, boat builder, but he rents it out through Oxnard realtor Leland Van Zandt. No note of who is living there at this moment."

"Copy that, thanks." Meyerstein looked at the driver. "ETA for us?"

The driver glanced at the GPS as they sped down the street. "Seven minutes."

"Goddamn!" said Meyerstein. "SWAT will have to make the call, as they'll be first on the ground. But approach with extreme caution."

Veitch replied, "Copy that. Out."

Meyerstein sensed the mood among the team she was traveling with had hardened. The focus had intensified. She knew that getting the terrorist cell, either dead or alive, was all that mattered.

But something was gnawing away at her. Her father had always instilled caution. She wondered about the sudden revelation of the GPS location.

She called Veitch, who picked up after one ring. "Martha, you still en route?"

Meyerstein peered at the road up ahead. "Yes. Listen, about the trace on the GPS signal . . ."

"What about it?"

"How come they've jammed their signals so far, but not this time?"

"Jamming technology works best when on the move. Indoors, it's more susceptible to interference from a TV cable box, or the wireless signal from a router."

Meyerstein pondered on that for a few moments. "Yeah, but what if it's something else?"

"What do you mean?"

"What if it's a trap—that's what I'm saying."

Veitch said nothing.

Meyerstein thought the silence went on too long. "I'm still waiting for a reply," she said. "We're nearly there, I need to know."

The driver said, "ETA two minutes."

"One of the analysts, Matty Sanders, thinks they're fucking with us," Veitch said.

"I know Matty. He's working counterterrorism for Homeland Security?"

"Yeah. Joint Counterterrorism Task Force. He believes these guys are out of the Quds loop, acting on their own, and they're fucking with us all. And he's convinced they won't stop until they get Reznick. He believes this little trip into Oxnard might just be a diversion. He said it might be a countersurveillance move, with them watching us."

"Tell him I want to talk when I get back," said Meyerstein.

"Will do, Martha, but the analysis is saying irrefutably it's them."

The sound of a chopper overhead was partially drowning out the conversation. "Let's hope you're right."

"I'm monitoring from the sky," said Veitch. "If they're there and make a run for it, we've got it covered."

"Keep this frequency open," replied Meyerstein.

"Will do."

Another voice came on the channel, from the SWAT vehicle approaching the house. "Ten seconds till arrival."

Meyerstein waited.

Thirty-Five

Reznick was sitting in a chair in the naval base interview room, when Belmont came in carrying two cups of coffee.

"How you holding up with this confinement, Jon?" he asked.

Reznick shrugged. "I'm holding up fine. Where's Meyerstein?"

Belmont handed him one of the cups. "Black, right?"

Reznick nodded and sipped some of the coffee. It felt good to get something apart from Dexedrine into his bloodstream.

"She's . . ." Belmont blew on his white coffee and sipped it. "She's in a meeting."

"This about the earlier call they put in?"

Belmont nodded.

"Meyerstein said that one of the guys is the brother of one of the scientists my team took out."

"I can't discuss that with you, Jon."

"Why the hell not?"

"Protocol."

"Protocol, huh? That's bullshit, General."

Belmont said nothing.

"Where do you work out of?" asked Reznick.

"I work for the government."

"The government."

"The American government." Belmont stared intently at him. "We need to nullify this threat—don't you agree, Jon?"

Reznick gulped down the rest of his coffee. "Yeah."

Belmont went across to the wall and leaned against it. "Jon, I want to level with you. We need to talk about options."

"Options?"

"Yeah—options, Jon."

Reznick sensed something wasn't right.

"But first, we're going to move you to a safer location."

"A safer location? What the hell does that mean?"

"Somewhere more secure."

Reznick didn't like the vibes he was picking up.

"Is Meyerstein happy with this, General?"

Belmont finished his coffee and lobbed the foam cup into the trash can. "Of course she is."

"What happens if I say I'm not going to play ball?"

"I think you will."

Reznick felt his eyes getting heavy and his mind foggy. "What was that?"

"I said I think you will."

Reznick closed his eyes for a second and struggled to open them again. His vision blurred, Belmont looming large as if through a fish-eye lens. He tried to speak but nothing came out.

"Are you OK, Jon?" Belmont's voice echoed, as if emanating from an underground chamber.

Everything went black.

Thirty-Six

The doors of the SWAT truck were flung open. A heavily armored team emerged and fanned out, encircling the property.

Meyerstein watched from the back seat of the SUV as the lead guy bounded up the stairs. She could hear his heavy breathing on her headset.

He knocked at the door.

Three more times he knocked. No reply.

His voice drawled, "Kick her in, son." His colleague stepped forward and kicked the door in, and the rest of the team stormed inside.

"FBI SWAT!" she heard them shout. "No one fucking move!"

Meyerstein could see the patterns of illumination inside the darkened house from the flashlights and helmet lights.

"FBI SWAT! Come out right now!"

Meyerstein held her breath for a few moments.

The lead guy was breathing hard. "Upstairs, downstairs, basement! All clear. Still to check the attic. Stand by."

Another SWAT voice: "GPS is showing it's here, the signal slap bang at this location. It's here. Get up into the attic."

"Yeah, we're on it."

A few moments later, a gruff voice said, "Yeah, it's been converted into a sleeping area. Unmade bed, piles of books lying around."

"Larry, check this out," a woman's voice said in the background.

Meyerstein felt her stomach tighten. She wondered why they couldn't find the cell phone.

"Larry," said the lead guy, "negative on the attic. We got a clean sweep?"

"One hundred percent clean, no sight or sound of these guys."

"Fuck!"

"GPS signal still shows it's right here in the house. Check drawers, cupboards, and every goddamn space if we have to. Tear off the walls. The cell phone is here. And we're not leaving until we find it."

"Yeah, copy that."

The search continued for the next eight minutes as Meyerstein listened in, hardly daring to breathe.

Then the radio silence was broken with the shrill sound of a cell phone ringing.

A voice said, "It's downstairs. Sounds like the kitchen."

It was in that terrible moment that Meyerstein realized what was about to happen.

She opened her mouth to shout instructions but it was too late. A huge explosion ripped through the house. Flames shot through the windows, as dust, glass, and masonry rained down on the cars outside.

Thirty-Seven

The seconds that followed were a blur for Meyerstein. Her driver reversed down the street as flames and secondary gas explosions erupted, turning the beachside community into a blazing war zone, debris strewn everywhere.

Meyerstein noticed a slight tremor in her hands as they headed back to base. "Son of a bitch!"

"Ma'am, are you OK?" a young FBI agent said.

"Forget about me, I'm fine. Oh God, what about the SWAT guys? Goddamn!"

Her cell phone rang, making her heart skip a beat. She sensed who it was going to be, and part of her didn't want to answer. But that wasn't an option.

"Who's this?"

"Assistant Director Meyerstein. I told you I'd call back."

Meyerstein seethed as the SUV picked up speed on the outskirts of Oxnard.

"We will find you. And we will kill you," she said furiously.

"I admire your bluster, Martha," he said. "Do you mind if I call you Martha?"

"Go to hell."

"It's just that I feel as if I know you now."

Meyerstein struggled to contain her fury. "You know nothing about me."

"Far from it. I know a great deal about you. Is your husband still with the beautiful young student? But then you still have your great career. Carved from your privileged background in the Chicago suburbs."

Her blood ran cold. "You'll pay for your barbarism."

"America could give a master class in barbarism. Carpet bombing children in Vietnam, Cambodia, and Laos with Agent Orange. Arming death squads across the world. Smuggling out Nazi scientists after the Second World War. Illegal war in Iraq. Do you want me to go on?"

"That's not the America that I know and love."

"Well that's the America we know and hate every day. The America that visits and imposes its structures and values, whether we want them or not, and all in the name of freedom. Do you think the Iraqis live in a free and democratic society after your intervention? Was the Shah of Iran a democrat? Do you know what his torturers did? Did you know what they did to my own father?"

Meyerstein closed her eyes. "Those SWAT guys have families. The people in the cinema had families. You're a monster. And don't blame America for your cold-blooded butchering of innocent people."

"I understand the hurt of families better than most, Martha. Mr. Reznick destroyed not only my brother that day. He destroyed me. Destroyed my other brother. And my sister. And my mother and father. So, here's what we want. You deliver Jon Reznick to us, and we can move on."

"So you can kill him?"

"What happens to Jon Reznick will be none of your concern."

"No."

"Maybe I'm not making myself sufficiently clear. If we don't have Jon Reznick delivered to us within the next twelve hours, we will kill many more Americans. And after that there will be more still. You will suffer. I'm sure you get the picture by now."

Meyerstein shook her head as the SUV approached the entrance to Point Mugu and was waved through. She knew she had to buy some time. "Delivered where?"

"We'll be in touch."

Meyerstein went straight through to the videoconference room, where Veitch and the other counterterrorism experts were waiting on the line.

"We intercepted the call again, easy as pie," he said.

"And?"

"And we have no location."

"What? They're running circles around us."

Veitch shook his head. "The NSA has their best guys working on this."

"What about launching a drone to try and detect the signal?"

"You're talking signal interception, right?"

"Absolutely. These new surveillance drones have the capability. They have direction-finding technology that can pinpoint the GPS location of cell phones or two-way radios, right?"

Veitch went quiet for a few moments. "I'll look into it."

"Prioritize it."

"I'm on it."

Meyerstein sighed. "I need to speak to Reznick before we decide our next move."

Veitch was silent. Meyerstein stared up at the screen and saw that he had averted his gaze.

"Am I missing something, guys?"

Veitch turned and looked at some of his colleagues before turning to face the screen. "Martha, I thought you knew."

"Knew? Knew what?"

"About Reznick."

"What about him?"

"Martha, Belmont and his guys have transferred him to a secure facility."

"On whose orders?"

"The National Security Council. We believe he's going to be flown from there to Tehran."

Thirty-Eight

Mohsen Sazegara was sitting in his motel room, the curtains drawn, watching Fox News on the small TV, when his cell phone rang.

"Who's this?"

"I have some news." The voice of Sosha Taremi, a Quds operative who was working with the Mexicans to trace Jimmy Rosen, who was hiding out in the Arizona desert.

"Tell me it's good news."

"He was very difficult to find. But we found him."

"Did Rosario help?"

"She was invaluable. She's with me now. Do you want to speak to her?"

"Not now. Tell me, where did you locate him?"

"He was out in the Sonoran Desert last night, shooting Mexicans. Tipping out their water. Leaving them to die."

"Nice guy. Where exactly?"

"On the Tohono O'odham Indian reservation, couple miles from the Mexican border."

"Anyone with him?"

"He was alone. We've heard that he got thrown out of his militia for knocking out the founder of the group."

"Has he been neutralized?"

Taremi cleared his throat. "I've got some footage for you to see. We wanted to get out of Arizona before we contacted you."

Mohsen's stomach tightened. "You got him?"

"I'll send you the clip," Taremi said before hanging up.

A few moments later, Mohsen's phone pinged as his inbox received a message. He opened the video attached, which showed Rosen kneeling in front of a shallow grave in the middle of the desert, hands on his head. A driver's license was shown to the camera—Jimmy Rosen's ID.

Mohsen felt his heart rate quicken as a gun was pressed to Rosen's head. There was a single shot, and the man fell backward into the grave. Mounds of sand were shoveled into the grave until it was filled.

A few minutes later, his phone rang.

"Fantastic work," said Mohsen.

"That only leaves one left—Reznick."

"He's mine."

Thirty-Nine

Reznick sensed he was not alone. He could hear whispered voices. He tried to open his eyes, and light suddenly burned his retinas. The background drone of a plane's engine. Vibrations. He heard someone move toward him.

"Mr. Reznick, apologies for the inconvenience, but needs must."

Reznick squinted as a towering figure came into focus. Shaved head, staring eyes.

"Where am I? What the hell's going on?"

"You're in transit."

"Who the hell are you?"

"That's classified," said the man, who was wearing military fatigues.

Reznick tried to get up, but plastic handcuffs attached to a steel ring on the floor restrained him. His mind flashed back to what had happened at the naval base. "Where's Belmont?"

"I don't know a Belmont."

"General Belmont, goddammit."

The soldier ignored him.

"Belmont!" Reznick shouted.

Nothing.

Reznick's hazy mind tried to figure out what had happened. "I want to speak to FBI Assistant Director Martha Meyerstein."

"That's not possible, Jon."

"Why not?"

The soldier ignored him again.

"What's your name and rank?"

The man smiled but said nothing.

"Who the fuck *are* you?" Reznick instinctively tried to get to his feet but the restraints kept him in place. "Goddammit, what are these for?"

"Just a precaution, Jon. So you don't hurt yourself."

A shudder of turbulence and Reznick's ears began to pop.

"Sit tight. We're landing in three minutes."

The man quickly moved forward and put a cloth over Reznick's nose. He felt himself slip, and was once again swallowed up by the darkness.

Forty

Jerry Morlach was staring through the floor-to-ceiling windows, as the setting sun over Los Angeles burned the sky a tangerine hue, when his phone rang. He lit up a cigarette and watched the smoke fill the room. He answered after the third ring. "Yeah?"

"Sorry for the delay." It was the man who had identified himself as the CIA contract worker.

"I was wondering when I was going to hear from you. Problem?"

"We've got the green light."

"Excellent. We can now get this over the line. What about the logistics?"

"Leave us to worry about that."

"Very well. If you insist."

Morlach dragged heavily on the cigarette and stepped out onto the terrace. "I need your word that there will be no last-minute change of plan."

"We're good to go at our end."

"Can I give an expected time of arrival?"

"You will have him within twenty-four hours."

"You work fast."

Morlach ended the call and crushed the cigarette out in an ashtray. He stared at the city's skyline, collecting his thoughts, then sent an encrypted SMS to his liaison man in Dubai, the most senior Iranian operative in the Middle East.

The lead has signed on.

Over the next hour, he fielded four separate encrypted calls as he was kept abreast of developments. Three calls came from the man in Dubai, and one direct from Tehran.

When everyone was satisfied that the necessary checks and balances were in place for the deal to go through, he sat down and lit another cigarette. He looked down on the City of Angels with a sense of satisfaction. Then he remembered the documents, which had arrived by FedEx, now carefully stored away in his safe.

The documents included fake passports, fake credit cards, and fake IDs for Mohsen Sazegara and his brother.

He felt uneasy with his role as a back channel to Tehran. If he had his way, he would never have agreed to the arrangement. But the CIA had made it known to him in no uncertain terms that he either did as he was told, or he would be deported back to Iran, no questions asked.

They had him by the balls. But he could live with that.

It was a small price to pay for his freedom.

Forty-One

When Reznick came to, he was in a huge windowless room, two air-conditioning units growling low in the background. He was strapped to a bolted-down steel chair, plastic cuffs on each ankle and wrist. There was a metallic aftertaste in his mouth. His brain felt fuzzy, he couldn't think straight. Where was he? Why was he here?

His memory was blank for a few moments. He tried to remember.

He knew he had a daughter. He could see her in his mind's eye. But he couldn't remember her goddamn name.

The room was cold, the walls flaking beige paint. There were scuff marks on the blue linoleum.

The sound of a door opening up behind him. He couldn't turn to see who was approaching. The click of a heavy lock. Footsteps getting closer.

In his peripheral vision he saw a silhouette. The man circled Reznick and stood about ten yards in front of him, arms folded. He looked familiar. But Reznick couldn't place him.

"Jon," the man said. "Do you remember my voice?"

It seemed very familiar. "Yeah, who are you?"

"General Belmont."

"Belmont?"

Belmont stared at Reznick for a few moments. "Is it coming back now?"

Reznick's brain was a rush of images, fractured memories. The sequence of events was starting to take on a semblance of order. "You . . . my coffee. You . . ."

"There was no other way, Jon."

Reznick said nothing, still trying to emerge fully from his drugged state. Fragmented thoughts flashed through his head.

"Four drops of chloral hydrate, and a few more on the plane."

"Where exactly am I?"

"You're underground in the Nevada desert. Short hop from California to here. Homey Airport—a remote part of Edwards Air Force Base."

"Groom Lake . . . Watertown Strip. Dreamland, right?"

Belmont smiled. "It's known by those names too, yes."

Reznick's mind was frantic with all the connected and interconnected parts of the last few days. The trip through the desert to California. The hit on Vincenza. The chase up into the hills over Malibu. The two Iranian-American students taken out by the sniper.

"Iran," he said.

"What about it?"

"I remember now."

"Do you?"

"Air Force base. Secrecy. You're going to fly me out and pass me on, aren't you?"

Belmont said nothing.

"The Iranians called Meyerstein. They want me. And they've turned the screw, am I right?"

"Maybe."

"What kind of officer are you?"

"The kind that acts in the national interest."

Reznick coughed, tasting chemical residue. He spat it out onto the lino floor.

"You look like shit," Belmont said.

"Thanks. Feel it, too. You gonna keep me here?"

"We're drawing up plans to perhaps move you up to Canada until this dies down."

"Then why am I being restrained?"

"It's a temporary measure. Keeps everyone safe."

Reznick stared at Belmont. "You're not taking me to Canada, are you?"

"We've still to finalize a few things. But it's important we keep you safe."

"You drug me, transport me to a desert bunker, chain me up, and now you say you're going to take me to Canada? For my own safety?"

"We have ways of doing things."

"You're going to fucking rendition me, aren't you? You're going to get me off your plate, and draw the heat away from those Quds guys who're still on the loose."

"I've been looking at your file, Jon. It makes interesting reading. Your cognitive skills, high intelligence, ability to compartmentalize your work but still maintain a relatively stable family background."

"You don't know the first thing about me."

"Oh, but I do."

"Is there a purpose to this?"

"Does there have to be a purpose, Jon?"

"Fuck your cod psychology."

"I didn't realize you had killed so many people."

Reznick said nothing.

"You just blend in . . . And your analytical skills are quite extraordinary."

"You wanna go on a date, General?"

Belmont gave a wry smile. "Problem with authority, they say."

"If you say so."

"Whatever you think—trust me, we're only interested in getting you to a safe place."

"Drugged, cuffed. You gotta do better than that, Belmont." Reznick looked around the room. "This is CIA."

"We only want to ensure that no one else suffers. I don't want you getting neutralized like your old Delta buddies."

"Tell me something, did you learn that lingo at the Farm in Virginia by any chance?"

"Jon, don't make this harder than it has to be. I don't like this any more than you do."

"So why don't you let me go?"

"I can't have you going AWOL on us."

"I know this place. Did it say that in my file?"

Belmont didn't respond.

"I know about the underground tunnels. I know the layout. I know what it looks like from the air. Trust me, it's not possible to go AWOL here."

Belmont cleared his throat. "Can I get you something to eat or drink?"

"Are you kidding me? After the last time?"

"Jon, that was purely a way to get you off that base with the minimum of fuss. I'm tasked with acting in everyone's best interests, including yours."

"That's very touching."

"Jon, I'm trying to help."

Reznick began to laugh. "Man, you're something else."

"What's so goddamn funny?"

Reznick ignored him.

"What's so goddamn funny, Reznick?"

Reznick shook his head, still laughing.

Belmont took a step forward. "I just want you to know that I admire the work you've done for our great country."

"Good for you, General."

"What the hell is wrong with you? That was a compliment, goddammit."

Reznick stared at him. "Am I making you uncomfortable, General?"

"I'm trying to be respectful."

"Bullshit. You don't give a fuck about me. But that's fine, because I sure as hell don't give a fuck about you or the CIA."

Belmont slapped Reznick hard around the face.

Reznick tasted blood. "That make you feel better, tough guy?"

"You're now the property of the United States government. Satisfied?"

"Funny, I thought I was an American citizen. A free man."

Reznick spat out some blood onto the floor.

Belmont took a step back. His face was flushed purple with rage. "You've crossed the line. I've been pretty reasonable up until now . . ."

Reznick began to laugh again.

"It didn't have to be like this."

"I've got news for you, General whatever-your-goddamn-name-is. I don't play your stupid fucking games. Neither does Meyerstein."

Belmont turned and left the room, switching the light off as he locked the deadbolts on the door.

Reznick was left alone in the darkness, cuffed to the cold metal chair.

Forty-Two

Meyerstein stood in the interview room facing Daniel Frostrop, the base commander. "On whose authority was Jon Reznick taken from here?"

"The Pentagon's."

"Tell me about Belmont and his role in this."

"Just after you left, an unregistered Gulfstream requested permission to land. They had CIA codes."

"Then what?"

"Six men, not in uniform, got out and entered the building. They left with Jon Reznick on a gurney, strapped in, unconscious."

Meyerstein felt her throat tighten. "What did you do about it?"

"I was in a meeting at the other end of the base."

"So the guys just give the right codes, land, take Reznick, and walk straight out again."

"General Belmont was in charge. He left with them. One of our guards challenged the group, but Belmont pulled rank."

Meyerstein turned her back on Frostrop for a few moments as she tried to regain her composure. "You'd think this was goddamn Guantanamo Bay."

The commander nodded.

"So where have they taken him?" she asked.

"No one knows. This is the way the CIA plays the game."

"I want to see the surveillance footage of this whole goddamn thing."

"That's not possible."

"What do you mean?"

"I've checked. There is no footage."

"Hang on, what are you talking about? I've seen the cameras all over this base. They must've captured every second."

Frostrop shook his head. "I've checked. Nothing."

"How come?"

"Jamming technology . . . or the system was hacked. No surveillance footage for the last twelve hours."

Meyerstein kicked over a metal trash can. "Son of a bitch."

"It's like they were never here," said the commander.

Twenty minutes later, Meyerstein hooked up again with Veitch and the FBI's counterterrorism team on a videoconferencing link.

"Who knew about this?" she asked.

"No one," replied Veitch. "It was CIA."

"What's going to happen to Reznick?"

Veitch sighed. "Tough call. The Director is preparing to call you any minute on this very subject."

A few moments later, one of the screens lit up, displaying the features of FBI Director O'Donoghue.

"Martha," he said, "this is out of our hands, I'm sorry."

"Who signed off on this?"

"The authorization goes to the very top."

"So we're just going to hand him over?"

"The wheels are in motion."

Meyerstein felt sick. "Where is he?"

"We don't know."

"I thought we were all on the same team, goddammit."

"Martha, all I know is that he's in a secure facility."

"And we're seriously just going to hand him over?"

"We've had assurance at the highest levels in Tehran that they will not harm him. But they will put him on trial. America will deny any knowledge or involvement. Official word will be that the operation was rogue. He'll go to jail."

Meyerstein bowed her head and closed her eyes. "They're going to kill him. You know that."

"Martha, this doesn't sit well with me. But our national interests come first."

"What about the hunt for the Iranian-American operatives?"

"What about it?"

"What if we find them first?"

O'Donoghue stared at her. "We only have a very narrow window until he's handed over."

"How long?"

"I don't know. Hours, perhaps," he said.

"Sir, we have two drones operating in Southern California as we speak."

"That's a long shot, Martha, and you know it."

"Listen, as long as they're up in the air, we have a chance."

O'Donoghue shook his head. "The odds aren't in our favor."

"This is shameful."

"That's enough, Martha."

"Sir, it *is* shameful. What the hell have we become?"

"What choice is there?" said O'Donoghue. "To allow massacres to go on indefinitely until we find them? Imagine the reaction of the American public if they find out that we could've done something to avert any future attacks."

"It's the wrong call, sir."

"Martha, it's the only call. This is for the good of America." O'Donoghue sighed. "You know Reznick personally, and that's what makes this so hard."

Meyerstein imagined Reznick alone in a Tehran prison—or worse, dead.

"Goddamn right it does."

Forty-Three

Reznick shuffled down a hallway, restrained at the wrists with plastic handcuffs, metal cuffs around his ankles. He noticed sheathed knives hanging from the belts of the four-man team surrounding him, as well as their 9mm handguns. He knew they were going to offload him. It was as clear as day.

He also knew where they were taking him. The remotest part of the facility, cut off from all the other areas, but linked by a series of underground corridors.

They walked past sullen guards, and the cameras constantly panning the area. Down a flight of stairs and into a huge communal shower room. His shoes were removed, then his socks. His clothes were cut off him, the cuffs kept on at all times.

He was photographed and strip-searched before he shuffled under the high-pressure shower. A towel was thrown at him, and Reznick dried himself off the best he could.

He was shown into an adjacent room, past a huge steel door with a serving hatch. He went inside, naked, cuffs still on. The door slammed shut.

Clothes were handed through the hatch in a brown paper bag.

A guard said, "Hands through the hatch."

Reznick complied and the plastic cuffs were cut off. The guard passed through a key. "You can now take off the ankle cuffs and hand them to us."

Reznick complied.

"Now get dressed," the guard said.

Reznick put on the new clothes. He felt stiff after having been restrained. He ran on the spot, followed by two hundred press-ups, then one hundred sit-ups.

The hatch opened. "Reznick, put your hands through. We need to put cuffs back on your wrists."

"Is that really necessary?"

"It's orders."

"From who?"

"General Belmont."

Reznick paced the room. "I don't think I'll bother. Thanks all the same."

"We need to put them on."

"Why?"

"He wants to speak to you, face to face."

"What about?"

"Flight up to Canada."

"And if I don't want to have the cuffs back on?"

"Then we'll have to do it for you." The voice was deadpan. Without a trace of emotion.

Reznick had learned early on that you only ever fight battles you can win. He placed his hands through the hatch and a set of plastic cuffs were tightened around his wrists, pinching the skin. "Easy, pal," he said.

The guard ignored him.

Reznick stepped back, cuffed hands in front of him.

"Can you head to the far corner of the room, Reznick?"

"What?"

"We need to put ankle cuffs on, too."

"What the fuck is this?"

"Reznick, we have orders. You know how it works."

Reznick took a step forward. The guard stared back, eyes dead.

"There's only one way we can do this, Reznick. And that's our way."

Reznick sensed the guard's mood was darkening by the second.

"Are you going to comply or not?"

"Why should I? To make your job easier? Because that would make my life more awkward. So, no, I'd rather not."

The guard sighed. "Is that your final answer?"

"I guess so."

The guard hesitated for a second. Then he raised a taser and fired through the hatch at Reznick's chest. Pain exploded through his body. He fell to the floor. The room went crazy as the pulses shocked his body. He wanted to scream. He felt himself losing control and began to convulse, writhing on the ground.

Forty-Four

Mohsen Sazegara stared out of the tinted passenger window of the SUV at the sun-drenched roads of the Hollywood Hills, and the towering palms shading the sidewalks. He felt his throat go dry as he thought ahead to the meeting with the reclusive man he'd never met.

The car hung a left, and then a right onto an affluent cul-de-sac.

Mohsen stared at the imposing, modernist glass house at the end of the road. "Straight ahead," he said.

The driver nodded and pulled up outside the gates, which were flanked by palms and a high wall. He pressed the intercom buzzer.

A few moments later a man's voice said, "Yes?"

"Here to collect a parcel," said the driver.

The gates opened and they drove through onto a beautifully paved driveway and down into a basement garage. Electronic doors closed behind them.

"I'll be five minutes," Mohsen said to the driver. "Wait here."

The driver nodded. "Yes sir."

Mohsen got out and headed toward a door, which was covered by three security cameras. He pressed the button next to it.

"Yes?" said the same voice.

"Here to collect the parcel."

"Can you give me the name of the person you should collect from?"

Mohsen knew the password. "Bill."

He was kept waiting for a little while. "Turn and look up at the camera to the right."

Mohsen turned and looked up as instructed. He wondered if it was face recognition software scanning his features.

"Good," the voice said. "Come on in. Bill can see you now."

The door was buzzed open and Mohsen went through. A burly man with a shaved head showed him to an airport-style body scanner. Mohsen stepped through, and then followed the man up two levels.

Once he got there, Mohsen looked around. Floor-to-ceiling windows overlooking LA. A pair of huge white sofas. Jazz playing low in the background.

"He'll be with you in a few minutes," said the burly man. "Take a seat, Mr. Sazegara."

Mohsen nodded, and took a seat on the sofa at a ninety-degree angle to the huge windows.

He waited for a few minutes, his heart pounding.

Then Mohsen heard a door open. He turned and saw a small man wearing tinted glasses, smoking a cigarette. It was Jerry Morlach.

Mohsen stood up.

Morlach smiled and shook his hand, motioning with his smoking hand for Mohsen to sit down. "Please," he said. He dragged heavily on the cigarette as plumes of smoke filled the room. "How are you?"

Mohsen felt a mixture of excitement and fear. "I'm OK, thank you."

Morlach looked at him and nodded.

"Thank you for seeing us at such short notice," said Mohsen.

Morlach's gaze drilled into Mohsen for a few moments. "I believe the original operation has morphed into something much more messy."

Mohsen felt his throat go dry with the smoke. "Mr. Morlach, we hit all the targets—"

"Bar one." Morlach cut him down quick.

Mohsen felt his pulse quicken again. Something about the guy unnerved him. Something intangible. "You've also attracted some attention . . . FBI, Homeland Security, National Security Council. In what was meant to be a low-key operation. A series of accidents."

Mohsen shifted in his seat.

"What happened to make it go so wrong?"

"Reznick. That's what happened."

"He came here to LA?"

Mohsen nodded, head bowed.

"He was trying to warn his old Delta friend, Blaine Vincenza, right before you took the man out?"

"Perhaps. He might've had the restaurant under surveillance, waiting to speak to Vincenza."

"Very messy. Look around you—I don't like messy. I like order."

Mohsen nodded.

"There are now ramifications . . . This makes things so much more complicated."

Mohsen opened his mouth to speak, but Morlach held up his hand to silence him. "Don't get me wrong," Morlach said. "You carried out the reprisals to the letter. But all this could have been avoided. When an operative starts becoming the news, you know we've fucked up."

Mohsen nodded, keen to appease him, realizing the futility of arguing. He knew Morlach was connected to the highest echelons of power in Tehran: the military, politicians, religious leaders. He was viewed by some as a mystic. By others as a dangerous man to know—someone who could get you killed with one call to the right person. It was said by some within the Quds Force that he was an American spy, a double agent. Others believed Morlach was in fact a former operative himself, his reputation forged during the revolution that had overthrown the Shah. Rumors also persisted that he had grown accustomed to a decadent lifestyle, with the private number of a Beverly Hills madam on speed dial.

Mohsen looked at Morlach, trying to push any negative thoughts to one side.

"Tell me," Morlach continued, "how do you think you will integrate back into Iranian society after living in Texas for so long?"

"It may take some time."

"It's a big move. How do you think your family will react?"

"My wife will miss the mall—but, hey, that's not such a loss. She shares my values. We both want to live a purer life."

Morlach smiled. "Indeed." He leaned over and stubbed his cigarette out in a glass ashtray on the coffee table, before walking over to the huge windows. "When I look out here, do you know what I see?"

"I'm not sure what you mean, sir."

"I see a city in chaos. A city without a soul. A city where the poor and the sick are left to die like dogs. A city that is choking with pollution, where the wealthy—like me—can afford to live above the smog line. Where politicians are bought and sold for campaign contribution funds from anonymous lobbyists. A city at war with itself. A city that is dying. But, paradoxically, a city where the fantasy of the American Dream is created and then spread around the world." He turned to look at Mohsen, hands behind his back. "How do you feel about America?"

"It sickens me."

Morlach nodded.

Mohsen stood up. "I appreciate your help and support." He held the man's hand and kissed the back of it.

Morlach leaned over and pressed a buzzer. His burly assistant came in and handed a backpack to Mohsen.

"It has everything you need. Brand-new American passport, new identity, driver's license, cash, credit cards, and return airline tickets, all under your new name, Charlie Thomas."

"I like that name. Sir, I can't thank you enough."

Morlach put his hand on Mohsen's shoulder. "They'll be watching LAX. My private plane will take you from Bob Hope Airport in Burbank. Gate A One. From there you will be flown to JFK. You will then catch a British Airways flight to London. And from there, a Lufthansa flight to Tehran with a stopover in Frankfurt."

Mohsen nodded.

"Police are at Bob Hope, don't get me wrong. But not in the same numbers, and certainly no Feds crawling around."

"I'm sorry we didn't complete the operation."

"You did very well. You are a hero."

Mohsen was fighting back tears.

"What about Jon Reznick?" he asked.

"He will be taken care of. Diplomatic channels are working overtime on this. Reznick will be on Iranian soil before you touch down in Tehran."

Forty-Five

The squeaking of heavy steel doors roused Reznick. Harsh artificial light flooded the windowless room. His head, neck, and back all ached. He couldn't stretch properly—his wrist and ankles were cuffed. Three guards approached, towering over him. They undid the ankle restraints binding him to the chair.

"You wanna take it easy, guys?" Reznick said.

The guards hauled him to his feet and out of the room. They took him down a series of corridors, deeper and deeper into the bowels of the top-secret facility. He became aware Belmont was now with them. Reznick heard his low voice in the background, directing operations.

"Take him to Room Seven A," said Belmont.

He saw a sign up ahead: *Intelligence Officers Only.* Beyond the sign, reinforced steel doors.

"Hold it right there," Belmont said.

Reznick stood still as Belmont brushed past. He watched as the brigadier general pressed his right index finger against a wall-mounted scanner and the doors opened.

They made their way down another corridor and stopped outside the seventh room on the left—7A.

Belmont pressed his index finger against another scanner. The door clicked open.

Reznick was pushed inside. He took in his surroundings. A dark-brown leather sofa, soft furnishings, muted lighting. He knew what it meant. They were trying to reassure him. But he knew it was bullshit. There was no reason to be at ease.

Belmont remained standing. "Take a seat, Jon," he said.

Reznick was hustled over to the sofa and pushed onto it.

Belmont turned to the guards. "Everything's fine now," he said. "Give me fifteen minutes. The plane's not ready to leave for another forty."

The guards turned and left, and the door closed behind them. Reznick noticed there was a fingerprint scanner on the inside as well. He also saw a high-visibility safety jacket hanging on a coat hook, and a pair of boots underneath.

Belmont folded his arms. "I'm sorry. I can only apologize."

Reznick said nothing.

"We've got all your Canadian documentation lined up. Ottawa is fully up to speed. And you're going to have a new identity up there. The downside is you won't be able to come back until this has died down—at least a year, maybe two."

Reznick winced.

"We'll get the cuffs off on the plane."

Reznick knew it was bullshit. He leaned forward and stared at the floor, hands still bound. "What else?"

"There's a house, by the water. Nova Scotia. I believe that's where your ancestors hailed from."

Reznick knew he wasn't going to Canada. There was no home by the water in Nova Scotia. He knew it would be a Gulfstream or Cessna used by a CIA front company, flown by CIA pilots, guarded by CIA guys, and then he'd be handed over. He knew about such deals. The rendition of Islamists to shithole, American-friendly countries in the Middle East.

As sure as night follows day, he knew the fate that would befall him: torture. Death would be his only escape. He thought of his daughter, alone in the world. But he knew she'd be looked after and protected by his late wife's father. And he knew Meyerstein would look after things, too. He wondered if she knew where he was.

"I read that your father fought in Vietnam," said Belmont. "The Marines."

Reznick nodded.

"So did my father. He wasn't so lucky. He didn't come back."

Reznick said nothing.

"War does terrible things to us. Makes us do terrible things." He sighed. "I believe you worked for the Agency, on and off?"

Reznick stared at Belmont.

"We never really leave its clutches, in all its guises. I was told that once. I think it's true."

The sound of a phone ringing.

Belmont reached into his pocket and pulled out his cell. He checked the caller ID and looked down at Reznick. "I need to take this." He pressed his finger against the scanner. The door opened and Belmont headed out into the hallway, leaving Reznick on his own.

Reznick's mind went into overdrive. He made a quick mental calculation, to see if he had enough time. This might be his last realistic opportunity.

He got off the sofa and went over to a pair of boots under the coat hook. He sat down, undid one of the Paracord laces and pulled it out. Then he made a bowline knot and slipped the loop around the front of his left shoe. He threaded the rest of the lace between the plastic cuffs, and tied another bowline knot and slipped the other side of the lace over his right foot. It was a move he hadn't practiced for two, maybe three years.

He thought he heard voices outside the room. Was it Belmont?

He began to pump his legs as if on a bike. Up, down, up, down, for maybe ten seconds, until the friction from the laces had severed the plastic cuffs on his wrists.

Reznick got up and sat back down on the sofa, hands tucked out of sight between his knees. A few moments later, the door opened and Belmont walked in.

"My apologies for the interruption," Belmont said. He walked over to a corner table and pulled a bottle of Scotch and a glass from a drawer. He poured a large measure, walked over to Reznick, and held the glass in front of him. "One for the road, Jon."

Reznick said nothing. But he was ready.

"What do you say?"

Reznick held his breath, not moving a muscle.

"I'm goddamn offering you a Scotch, Reznick!" Belmont snapped.

Reznick stared at him wordlessly.

"I said—"

Reznick sprung up from the sofa and grabbed Belmont by the throat, slamming him to the ground. Then he smashed his fist into Belmont's jaw. There was a terrible crack and Belmont lay motionless, unconscious.

Reznick's blood was pumping. He ripped off his clothes, and stripped Belmont of his. He saw that the brigadier general had a sheathed knife on the back of his belt and a 9mm under his jacket. He pulled on the clothes, and did up the belt with the knife nice and tight. It was a pretty good fit. Average-size guy. He checked the jacket pocket: cell phone, sunglasses, photo ID.

He began to think ahead to his escape. He ripped up the clothes he had discarded, and rammed part of his torn shirt in Belmont's mouth.

Belmont started to come around. Reznick pressed a hand over his gagged mouth, then pushed one knee into his chest and the other on top of his right arm. The brigadier general's eyes opened wide and he tried to scream. But it came out muffled.

Reznick pulled out the knife and cut off Belmont's index finger. The cold steel easily sliced through the bone. Belmont's face turned white as his blood spilled onto the floor. Reznick punched him hard on the temple and he was out cold again.

Reznick picked up the bleeding, still-warm finger and walked over to the scanner. He pressed the severed fingertip hard against it. A green pinprick of light appeared on the scanner, and the door mechanism clicked. He dropped the severed finger and pushed open the door.

The corridor was empty.

Reznick turned left. At the end of the hallway, there was a room marked *Aircraft Maintenance Crew Only*. Reznick pushed open the door. Inside were rows of lockers. He opened a few. Then he turned and saw a uniformed guard staring at him, gun drawn.

"Where's your ID?" the man said.

"Sorry, first day," Reznick said. He reached into his inside pocket and took out the ID card, then walked toward the guard. "Here's my identification."

The guard stared at the ID Reznick held in his hand. Then his radio crackled, distracting him.

Reznick punched the guard hard in the neck before he had time to react. The guard dropped to the ground, head cracking on the floor. Reznick took off the guard's gray uniform and shoes. The shoes were half a size too small, but they'd have to do. Uniform was a fraction big, but he pulled it over Belmont's clothes and it bulked him out nicely.

He took the guard's ID, hanging it around his neck.

Reznick was back in the zone. He walked back into the locker room and noticed a smoke alarm. Rifling through the guard's pockets, he found some cigarettes and a lighter.

He pulled all the toilet rolls and paper towels from the washroom, threw them into a trash can, and placed it directly underneath the sensor. Then he set fire to it and headed out the door.

Down an adjacent corridor was a door marked *Aircraft Maintenance Hangar—Authorized Personnel Only.* Reznick pushed it open. Inside, a guy on scaffolding was spray-painting a small plane, and three mechanics were working on an engine.

Suddenly, fire alarms blared out all around.

Reznick's heart was pumping hard. He followed the men out an emergency exit into the cool night. On the airfield outside, a guy in blue overalls driving a golf buggy approached the group, and Reznick put up his hand as if to stop him.

The buggy slowed to a halt.

Reznick said, "Got a fire situation, buddy. Need to borrow this to alert the security gate."

The maintenance guy jumped out.

"Where's the nearest gate?" asked Reznick.

The guy shrugged. "Don't you know?"

"Just been transferred."

The man pointed northwest. "Gate Three A, two hundred yards on the right."

Reznick jumped into the buggy and drove onto the floodlit roadways in the direction of the security gate.

An armed guard stepped forward.

"We've got a fire in basement level four," said Reznick.

"So I heard," replied the guard. "What are you doing here?"

Reznick got out of the golf buggy and showed the guard his ID.

"I'm McIlroy," he said.

The guard put his hand out to take the ID. Reznick smashed a fist into the guy's jaw and he fell back, his head striking the concrete. Out cold.

Reznick bent over, rifled in the guard's pockets, and pulled out a set of car keys. He was in luck. He ran to the nearest parking lot and pressed the fob. A Jeep's lights flashed as the alarm deactivated. He climbed in, slammed the door shut, and switched on the air conditioning. Then he drove out of the facility and headed into the Nevada desert.

Forty-Six

Veitch relayed the news about Reznick's escape to Meyerstein from one of the big screens in the videoconference room. She stared up at him in disbelief.

"How is that possible?" she asked. "Are we sure he's escaped?"

"Apparently so."

"What sort of bullshit is that?"

"The sort of bullshit that happens when Langley gets involved." Meyerstein sighed. "They shouldn't have tried to hand him over to the Iranians."

"Not surprisingly, the CIA is saying nothing."

"What about Belmont?"

"What about him?"

"What's the latest?"

"Lost a lot of blood. They're trying to reattach the finger and rebuild his nose."

"What a fuck-up," she said.

"Indeed."

"Does the President know about this?"

"He does now."

"What are his people saying?"

Veitch sighed. "They think Reznick is out of control. If they catch him, there's a good chance they might just neutralize him. This is bad."

"I need time to see where we go from here. We'll talk in fifteen minutes." She ended the video call and headed to the bathroom.

She felt conflicted. If she was honest with herself, she was relieved Reznick wasn't on his way to Tehran. But there was the possibility of blowback from the Iranians once they realized the Reznick deal was dead in the water. She splashed cold water on her face, looked in the mirror, and saw bloodshot eyes staring back at her. The lack of sleep and the pressure were catching up with her. She looked a mess. But that was nothing compared to the situation she faced with Reznick hacking off Brigadier General Belmont's finger and going AWOL.

She pulled out some face wipes from her handbag and removed her makeup. Then she applied red lipstick, and lots of Touche Éclat to cover up the shadows under her eyes. Brushed her hair. An improvement, at least.

But she still felt swamped. Pulled in a million different directions.

Meyerstein tried to gather her thoughts. She'd been awake for the best part of twenty-four hours and was dog-tired. Her head was swimming in a deluge of information. Assessment, analysis, hybrid-threat appraisals, irregular warfare tactical briefings . . . On it went.

Her phone vibrated. A unfamiliar number.

Meyerstein pressed the green button, expecting to hear the American-Iranian. "Yes?"

She sensed someone was on the other end, although they weren't saying anything. She thought she heard traffic in the distance.

"Who's this?" she said.

"Meyerstein . . ."

It was Reznick.

"Jon . . ."

"What did you know about where Belmont was taking me?"

"I knew nothing."

"Nothing?"

"Listen to me, I only discovered you'd been taken when I returned from Oxnard."

"How do I know you're telling the truth?"

"Do you think I'm lying?"

A long pause. "No, I don't."

Meyerstein sighed. "Jon, a lot has happened. Stuff you don't know about. You have to come in."

"I'm sorry, I don't follow."

Meyerstein told him about the chemical attack in the cinema, and the booby-trapped house and the FBI SWAT team. "That's why Belmont wanted to offload you."

"I was told they were taking me to Canada."

"That's a lie."

"Yeah, no kidding."

"Jon, you need to come in."

"No deal."

"Jon, you need to see sense."

"I've had my fill of sense. Now I'm going to do things my way."

"What can I say that would make you change your mind?"

"It's too late."

"Jon, you need to keep me in on this—"

The line went dead.

A minute later, Veitch called from McLean. "Martha, we got the call."

"Where is he?"

"The signal popped up just for a brief moment."

"Location?"

"He's headed for LA."

Forty-Seven

Reznick was driving west on Sunset Boulevard after robbing a downtown pharmacist of some cash and Dexedrine. Seeing a sign for a bar, he cut across the lanes and pulled up at a parking lot opposite. He walked into the bar and ordered a Heineken.

Pulling out the pharmacist's wallet, he gave the barman a twenty-dollar bill, ordered some pizza, and asked if he could use the phone. The barman shrugged. "Go right ahead, buddy," he said. "Pizza will be with you in a few."

Reznick picked up the phone and turned his back on the barman. He punched in the number of a guy he knew in Nebraska, Bobby Haines. His brother had been in Delta alongside Reznick.

The phone rang twice before being picked up. "Bob, I don't know if you remember me," he said quickly. "It's Jon Reznick."

A long silence. "Hey, Jon, how the hell are you?"

"Yeah, look, I need a favor. And we need to keep it low-key."

"Name it."

"It's of the fast-turnaround variety."

"I'm listening."

"I've got a cell phone number. I want an address for it."

"I use an intermediary these days. It'll cost you."

"How much?"

"Couple hundred bucks."

"I'll wire it to you in the next twenty-four hours. I need this now."

"You got it, Jon. I've got the number you're calling from. Gimme the cell phone you're trying to trace the billing address for."

Reznick gave him the number.

"Leave it with me," Haines said before he hung up.

Reznick sat down on a stool.

The barman looked at Reznick. "Just passing through?"

"Yeah, pretty much," Reznick said, taking a large bite out of the pizza. It felt good to get food inside him.

"I couldn't help hearing that you were looking for an address. You a cop or a PI, man? It's cool, it's not a problem."

Reznick said nothing as he ate. He always found it best not to let on.

"I used to be LAPD, many years back," said the barman, patting his belly. "Got shot in the stomach." He lifted his T-shirt and showed Reznick a small scar. "Some thug, six blocks from here."

Reznick nodded.

"The thing is," the barman said, "I was lucky. My buddy got shot up bad. Lost his fucking eye. You believe that shit? And all because we stopped the guy for erratic driving." He shook his head. "It ain't right. Fucker skipped bail. You believe they gave him bail? You couldn't make shit like that up."

The bar phone rang and Reznick grabbed it before the barman could.

"Jon, this is proving to be tricky," said Haines.

"How come?"

"Don't want to elaborate, but usually my guy's able to pull up cell phone billing addresses pretty easy."

"What are you saying?"

"I'm saying I need time."

"How long?"

"An hour."

Reznick weighed up his options. "I'll call you in an hour," he said. Then he handed the phone back to the barman. "Appreciate that."

"Hey, any time."

Reznick tipped the guy twenty dollars and left the bar, heading along Sunset Boulevard on foot.

Ten minutes later, he was in West Hollywood. Hipsters and a younger crowd milling around. He walked on and ended up at the Power House bar. A vertical neon-lit sign. A huge slab of a doorman standing outside, staring straight ahead. Reznick nodded as he brushed past the guy.

Inside, it was suitably dark. A handful of bikers sitting down at the far end of the bar. A stoned kid sitting alone in a booth, giggling. The jukebox was playing Tom Petty. Loud.

Reznick bought a Heineken and sat at the bar. The barman was smoking as he wiped down the counter.

Reznick stared at the bottles of blended Scotch behind the bar. He was tempted just to sit where he was and not go anywhere. Just drink, and forget. The dark thoughts lingered as he sat in the dingy bar, the stench of smoke and spilled booze seeping through his pores.

He went to the filthy toilet, emptied his bladder, and washed his hands. When he returned to his seat, the barman had opened a fresh bottle of beer. "You looked like you needed another, man."

Reznick nodded. The jukebox was now playing some blues song. Maybe Muddy Waters. He handed the barman a twenty-dollar bill. "You got a phone I could use? Lost my goddamn cell this evening."

The barman took the money and handed him his cell phone. "Go right ahead."

Reznick took the phone and punched in Bobby Haines's number. It rang for almost a minute.

"Jon, sorry, just got back in."

"Any luck?"

"Second time lucky. It's in LA, all right. Hollywood Hills West. Where are you now?"

"A bar in West Hollywood."

"You're not far. The address you're looking for is eighty-five nineteen Hedges Place."

Reznick made a mental note.

"Swanky three-million-dollar homes there. Nice part of town."

"Anything I should worry about?"

"Cops crawling all over the locale. Be careful."

"Anything else?"

"The property is owned by a Jerry Morlach. Aged seventy-eight. Phone is registered to one of his companies, Entertainment Finance LA. Big shot."

Reznick said, "How far on foot?"

"Three miles, give or take. West and then up into the Hills. Best bet is to take a cab. Don't do it on foot. Like I said, cops prowling about everywhere around there."

"How do you know?"

"How do I know what?"

"That cops are prowling everywhere?"

"LAPD police scanner. Got a live feed from the Internet. They even mentioned your name."

Reznick didn't react.

"Stay safe."

Reznick hung up. He finished the rest of his beer and headed out the rear exit, past a beaten-up patio full of smokers. He climbed over the rear wall, and no one said a thing.

Then he headed down a deserted side street and hotwired a parked tow truck.

Reznick got back onto Sunset and headed west. He stopped off at a corner store and bought a cheap, pay-as-you-go phone. He got back in the truck and punched Morlach's address into the vehicle's satnav. It guided him through West Hollywood— past nail bars, sky bars, restaurants, clubs, shops.

The satnav told Reznick to turn right, and he drove up Queens Road and then left onto Miller Drive, past multimillion-dollar homes. The vast, sulfurous glow of the city spread out below.

As the GPS led him on to Hedges Place, the road became a cul-de-sac. The last house was surrounded by a huge stone wall. Reznick spotted a wooden door with a metal panel for the intercom. Adjacent was an electronically controlled iron gate.

He took a few moments to run through the options in his head. There were a few houses overlooking the front—and almost certainly more houses to the rear of Morlach's property.

Next to him, on the truck's passenger seat, was a clipboard with some paperwork attached. He edged forward to the gate, pulled the handbrake, and switched the engine off. He picked up the clipboard and got out of the truck. He pressed the buzzer and put the cell phone to his ear as he pretended to talk. The face of a heavyset guy flashed up on the small screen.

"Hey, buddy, I'm here to pick up the vehicle that was involved in the freeway scrape earlier."

"I'm sorry, who are you?"

"Eighty-five nineteen Hedge Place. I've got the right address?"

"I don't know anything about this."

"Buddy, I've just had my boss on the phone, busting my balls. No way I'm going back to the depot without that vehicle."

"Look, I'll be right down."

Reznick stood with his back to the door, waiting for the man to appear. The door opened and the guy stepped forward.

"What's this about?"

Reznick turned around and smashed his fist into the side of the guy's neck. He went down unconscious. Reznick frisked him. Underneath the man's loose-fitting shirt was a 9mm Glock strapped to his waistband. He pulled the man over to the back of the truck, tied an old rag around his mouth, trussed him up with tow straps, and removed the Glock.

The man would be out of it for a good ten minutes, maybe more.

Reznick headed through the open door into a huge hall. He could hear a TV. He followed the sound into a spacious living room. Floor-to-ceiling views of LA.

But he could also hear something else. A faint sound. It was coming from upstairs.

Reznick padded up the carpeted steps. He heard a man's voice, talking on the phone. Reznick held his breath as he crept toward the closed door. He listened for a few moments, until the man on the other side ended the call. Then he opened the door and walked in.

Reznick pointed his gun at the man sitting on the bed. "This is how it's going to work—I talk, you listen."

The man sat there, frozen.

Reznick picked up the man's phone from the nightstand. "Is this yours?"

The man nodded.

Reznick scrolled through the call history. "I see you've been in contact with General Belmont."

The man closed his eyes.

"Tell me about that."

"I don't know what you mean."

"Cut the crap."

The man's lower lip began to quiver. "Please, who are you? Where is my assistant, Pravi?"

"You need to listen. I asked you a question. Tell me about how you know General Belmont."

"I don't know a General Belmont."

Reznick showed Belmont's number to the man. "Tell me about this call. Who is this?"

The man ignored him.

Reznick pulled back the slide on his gun.

The man stared at Reznick. "You're him, aren't you? You're Reznick."

"Last chance. Who is this guy you called? Is he one of the people after me?"

"He's a guy I do business with."

"Quds?"

"I don't know what you're talking about."

"Where is he?"

The man didn't respond.

Reznick grabbed him by the throat and pressed the gun to his forehead.

"You're starting to fucking annoy me. Now where is he?"

The man reached under a pillow. "Maybe this can—"

Reznick caught a glimpse of black metal. He didn't hesitate. He pulled the trigger.

Blood and gray fragments of brain matter splattered onto the wall. Then ear-splitting, sound-activated alarms went off all around the house.

Forty-Eight

Meyerstein was strapped into the back seat of an FBI chopper as it swooped low over the Hollywood Hills, searchlights strafing the backyards and pools of luxury mansions. Suddenly, Stamper's voice sounded in her headset.

"Martha, it's Roy."

"Talk to me, Roy. This better be good news."

"It's all bad. Reznick's been classified a high-risk security threat. Shoot on sight. God knows where it'll end."

"That's bullshit. We need to find out where he is."

"Martha, we have nothing. It's like Reznick's a ghost. He's just vanished."

The helicopter banked right and headed higher into the hills above Los Angeles. "What do we know about this Morlach guy and his relationship with Belmont?"

"The CIA is saying nothing. But people I know say that Belmont works out of the Pentagon and on regime-change stuff down at The Farm in Virginia."

"You know as well as I do, Roy, how they operate. Denial . . . deflection. It's been like that since forever."

Stamper sighed down the line.

Meyerstein adjusted her headset. "What about the drones looking for the Iranians?"

"Nothing. They're playing us."

"What about Reznick? What was the last sighting?"

"Security footage. On foot, heading up high into the Hollywood Hills. Cops are trawling the area with dogs and night-vision equipment. And they're deploying heat-seeking imaging equipment, just like we are."

Meyerstein stared down at the slow-moving traffic on Sunset Boulevard, and the neon lights shimmering in the darkness. The helicopter's headlights illuminated the scrub below. "I haven't heard from the Iranian contact. Is he waiting for a message from Tehran? Has he gone to ground? A safe house? Is he waiting for our next move?"

"The problem is, if this guy—or these guys—get to hear that Reznick is not en route to Tehran, then we really are in trouble. We're at their mercy."

"We're at nobody's mercy, Roy. We need to find these sons of bitches. And quick."

"What about Reznick?"

"Him too."

"Martha, I've said this before, and I'll say it again. He's a liability."

"Roy, do you listen to yourself sometimes?"

Stamper said nothing.

"We were going to send him to Iran. That was the wrong call."

"Martha, it was the only call which could be made. What Reznick did—"

"You mean save himself? Because that's what he did. He knew he wasn't getting transferred up to Canada."

"Is that what they said they were doing?" asked Stamper.

"That was the bullshit story Belmont concocted. Reznick would have seen through that."

The pilot signaled to her.

"Roy, speak soon." She turned to the pilot. "Yeah, what've you got?"

"Call coming through to you from Special Agent Veitch in McLean."

"Put him on."

"We just picked up a live signal thirty seconds ago." Veitch's voice was clear in her ears. "He's on the Hollywood Freeway."

"Reznick?"

"We think so."

Meyerstein signaled for the pilot to head in that direction. "Copy that, we're on our way."

"You need to know, Martha . . . Morlach was a diplomatic back channel to Tehran for the American government."

Meyerstein felt her insides churn. "And Reznick has just killed him?"

"In cold blood."

Meyerstein stared down at the lights of the cars on the freeway, a sinking feeling in her stomach.

Forty-Nine

Reznick headed off the freeway, and drove until he found an underground parking lot. He pulled out the cell he had taken from Morlach's home and downloaded the mSpy app. The tracking software would help him locate his next target.

Then he texted a message to the last number Morlach had dialed. *You must call me.*

A few moments later, the phone rang. On the sixth ring, Reznick answered.

"I'm responding to your message," said the voice on the line.

Reznick remained silent and ended the call. He had what he wanted.

The GPS information flashed up on the cell: Bob Hope Airport in Burbank. It had been a long shot, but the man who had called Morlach last hadn't switched off the GPS on his phone.

Reznick's heart rate hiked up a notch. He sent another message. *Can't speak on the phone. Where can I meet you at airport?*

A few moments later, a text came in.

Directly outside Terminal A.

Reznick sent a text back: *See you in half an hour. New paperwork.*

He then took the battery and the SIM card out of the cell, and dropped them both down a storm drain. Then he strode across to a nearby BMW convertible, opened up the hood, ripped out the alarm wiring, and started it up.

Reznick revved the engine and programmed Bob Hope Airport into the car's satnav. He was seven miles from his location—a matter of minutes up the freeway.

Fifty

Mohsen's senses were working overtime as he sat drinking a scalding-hot coffee in the tacky terminal of Bob Hope Airport in Burbank. He watched as a young man wiped down a nearby table, and wondered about the messages from Morlach. He didn't like it.

He went over to a payphone and caught sight of his brother—who had arrived a few minutes after him—pretending to read the *LA Times*. He punched in a number, popped in a couple of bucks, and waited until he heard the familiar voice of his handler.

"I'm glad you called," the voice said before Mohsen could speak.

"I'm looking for clarification."

"Your father has gone." The coded message meant: *Morlach is dead.*

"I just received a call."

"It's Reznick."

Mohsen went quiet for a few moments. "I see. How do you know it's him?"

"Never mind. He's not far. But you have one thing in your favor."

"And what's that?"

"Reznick doesn't know there are two of you. And he doesn't know what either of you look like."

"We'll handle him, don't worry."

"We need to make sure this time."

"It's done."

Mohsen ended the conversation and called Jorge Garcia's number.

"Mo, I believe things are not so good at your end."

"I'm looking for a way out . . . Is everything in place?"

"Rosario is very near you."

"Where?"

"She's waiting at the Ramada Inn, Burbank. The shuttle bus from the airport will take you there. Rosario knows what to do. You have my word."

"Thank you, my friend."

The line went dead.

Mohsen called his brother. "Restroom nearest to you in two minutes."

He hung up and walked over to the bathroom. He'd just finished checking the stalls were all empty when his brother came in.

Mohsen put a finger to his lips and whispered, "Dismantle your phone—take out your battery and SIM card. Flush them away."

His brother went into the first stall and did as instructed. Mohsen did the same.

"He's coming here," said Mohsen.

"What?"

"Reznick is on his way here."

"How is that possible?"

"It just is." Mohsen could see the burning hurt in his brother's eyes.

"I thought he was being traded in exchange for us stopping any further terrorist attacks."

"That was the plan. But it's all gone wrong. And he's on to us. So we need to take care of him."

"What's he expecting?"

"An Iranian standing directly outside Terminal A."

Behzad cleared his throat. "I'm not having that. I'm going to be the one."

Mohsen sighed. He knew his brother was headstrong. Impulsive. Consumed by a dark anger. Mohsen, by contrast, had learned to push the bad thoughts aside as and when required. He still grieved for his brother, but he had chosen to remember his brother full of life and promise. A passionate and brilliant man.

The more he thought about it, the more he realized that he could compartmentalize it so much better than Behzad. His brother only lived to avenge their elder brother. Mohsen understood. But he knew the mission needed focus. And discipline.

"I will be the sacrifice," Behzad whispered. "But you must promise me you will kill Reznick."

"I give you my solemn word," said Mohsen. "He will die."

Fifty-One

As Reznick drove hard toward Burbank, he called up Bobby Haines.

"What's going on, Jon?"

"I need something else."

"What're you looking for, bro?"

"A gun shop in or around Burbank, open right now."

A few moments' pause. "Guns and Stuff, ninety-three seventy-six West Magnolia Boulevard, Unit Seven."

"Owe you one." Reznick ended the call and entered the details into the satnav. Six minutes later, he was in downtown Burbank. He pulled up on a side street, outside a children's clothing store. He crossed the street into the gun shop and looked at the racks of weapons.

The tattooed guy behind the counter grinned. "Heading out to the range late tonight, buddy?"

"Just new in town. I'm looking to see if you can help me."

The guy shrugged. "What you looking for?"

"Two things. The best sniper rifle you've got, and night-vision sights."

"Night hunter, right?"

"Oh yeah."

"Love that. OK, here's what we've got."

The guy went down the racks and picked out a mean-looking rifle. "Just got a load of these in. M24. All-American, classic sniper rifle."

Reznick held it and looked down the scope. "Good weight, balance."

"You know your guns. Bolt action. As used by the US Army. But I guess you knew that already. The M24 uses the Remington 700 action. The stock is composite Kevlar, graphite—just the best. Bipod is detachable. I've got some armor-piercing ammo which might interest you."

"Indeed it does." Reznick stared down the scope again. It was perfect.

The guy handed him a box. "Telescopic sights. Same gear used by Seals and Delta."

Reznick nodded. "How much for it all, including the ammo?"

"Thirty-seven hundred for the rifle. For the telescopic scopes, another two big ones. Ammo, maybe another grand, which should keep you going. But, hey, I can give you the whole thing for six thousand dollars."

"You got it."

The guy grinned. "Man, I love it when a customer just knows what they want," he said.

"I'm also looking for a Beretta 9mm with ammo," said Reznick.

"That's a good gun." He bent down and pulled out a tray of handguns. He chose a pristine Beretta, picked it up as if he were handling a gold bar, and handed it over to Reznick.

Reznick pulled back the slide and stared down the barrel.

"That's a good gun, my friend," the guy said.

Reznick nodded. "And military-grade binoculars?"

The guy bent over, unlocked a drawer, and handed him a pair of expensive-looking binoculars. "You're really going for it, aren't you? OK, these were imported from Germany last month. Straight out the box."

"Ammo for the Beretta?"

The guy pulled out four packets of magazine ammo. Reznick picked up one packet, opened it, and slid a magazine into the gun.

The guy held up his hands. "Hey, buddy, that's absolutely not allowed."

Reznick flicked off the safety and pointed the gun at the guy's head. "Don't fucking move."

The guy closed his eyes.

"OK, this is how it's gonna work. I want you to very carefully deactivate the security cameras and alarm system. Comprendi?"

The guy nodded hard. He opened up a panel on the wall behind him and flicked a couple of switches. "We're offline now."

"You sure?"

"Alarms are all off, I swear on my mother's life."

"Don't worry, I'll pay you. Just not now."

Reznick ordered the man into the stockroom, where he tied him up with duct tape and string, and locked the guy inside. Then he threw the ammo, rifle, gun, and binoculars into a black nylon rifle case he took from a shelf. He got back in the car, lifted up the rear seating, and slid in the bag to keep it out of view, before heading straight for the airport.

He thought about Tiny in Falluja. Then the tears in Pete Dorfman's eyes as he'd stared into his drink.

It was time.

Fifty-Two

Meyerstein's chopper landed in the parking lot of a mall just off the freeway. She jumped out and climbed into a waiting SUV. Roy Stamper was already sitting on the back seat.

"So where the hell is he?" she said, buckling up. "He can't just have vanished."

"The NSA says the signal died less than a mile from here."

"He was heading north at the time, right?"

"Due north on the Hollywood Freeway. That's all we have."

Meyerstein was handed an iPad and pulled up Google Maps. "He's in North Hollywood. The Ventura Freeway's nearby. His options are unlimited."

"Pretty much. That is if he's looking to escape. I'm not so sure that's what he has in mind."

Meyerstein thought of that for a moment as she rubbed her eyes. "Veitch was running the scenarios. What's the latest?"

"Last time I tried to speak to him, he was incommunicado," said Stamper.

Meyerstein inputted the unlisted number for Veitch into her cell.

"Martha," said Veitch, sounding harassed, "we're on it."

"I need you to find him—now. I don't need excuses."

"Martha, gimme a break. These things take time."

"We're out of time. I also want more intel on Morlach."

"We're reaching out to the CIA on this. They have some classified material on him that I haven't got access to at this stage."

Meyerstein slammed her fist into the seat in front. "Are you kidding me?"

"We're working our way through this. We're getting there."

"Give me what you've got."

Veitch sighed down the phone. "Morlach's estimated worth is two hundred and forty-nine million dollars. He's a big spender. Top-of-the-line cars—"

"What else? Who's looking over this? Give me a name."

"Special Agent Sarah Munro."

"Get her to call me right away."

A few moments later, Munro was on the line. "Ma'am, how can I help? I'm sifting through Morlach's finances and outgoings as we speak."

"Tell me what you've got, Sarah."

"As well as his thing for upscale cars, he's bought a couple of trendy restaurants in Hollywood."

"Sarah, I don't mean to be tetchy, but I'm looking for anything unusual about the expenditure," said Meyerstein.

"Got it. He's a very wealthy man. Buys big presents for himself and friends. This is Hollywood."

"But what else? I want to know about unusual patterns of spending. Do you see what I'm getting at?"

"Ma'am, I'm compiling the report, but I'm nowhere near—"

"Special Agent Munro, listen to me. Give me what you've got. Not tomorrow, not in an hour. I want it now. What do you know *now*?"

"There is something that caught my eye," said Munro.

"What?"

"Morlach doesn't like splashing out on flights."

"How do you mean?"

"Well, instead of flying first-class from LAX to New York, he's taken dozens of flights on a budget airline—Jet Blue."

"Not a clincher for me."

"But what if I told you he owns a Cessna based at Bob Hope Airport in Burbank?"

Meyerstein took a few moments to absorb the information. "Call me back if anything else emerges." She ended the call, turned to Stamper, and relayed the information to him. "Morlach was the on-the-ground link between this Quds crew and Tehran. He was also a back channel used by the CIA. And he has a goddamn Cessna at Burbank."

Stamper shrugged. "So?"

"FBI cover at Burbank, if memory serves me, is nonexistent. Compare and contrast with LAX. Think about it—Burbank has minimal Feds and cops. Internal commuter stuff, not international."

Stamper nodded.

"What if Morlach has been using this route because he knows, or has been told, that it's less likely to attract the attention that a hub airport with international connections would have?"

"I see where you're going with this."

Just then, Meyerstein's phone rang.

"Ma'am, it's Veitch. We got something."

"What is it?"

"Text message sent by Reznick to an unknown number. And we've pinpointed the GPS location of the recipient to Bob Hope Airport."

"When?"

"Eight minutes ago."

"Great work." She tapped the driver on the shoulder. "Bob Hope Airport, Burbank. Move it!"

Fifty-Three

Reznick slowed down as he approached the short-stay parking garage. He glanced across at the terminal building opposite. A few travelers with backpacks, others pulling trunks on wheels. All Caucasian.

He pulled up at the security barrier.

The guard stepped forward. "Evening, sir. Can you drive through and park it up on the left?" he said. "We need to have a look inside your car."

Reznick nodded and drove over to the designated vehicle-screening area.

He stepped out of the car. "Be my guest."

"You mind opening the trunk?"

Reznick did as he was told. The guard poked a flashlight inside and took a cursory look.

"That's fine, sir," he said. "You picking up?"

Reznick nodded. "I'm a bit early. Picking up my sister."

"Two hours waiting, max."

"That's fine, she's due in around an hour."

Reznick got back in his vehicle and drove to the top of the four-story car park. He parked at the far end, a distance away from the nearest vehicle. He checked the line of sight and saw it overlooked the terminal building. He shut off the engine and pulled the bag out from underneath the rear seat. Then he quickly assembled the rifle, inserted the magazine, and attached the night-vision scope. He placed it on the floor and picked up the night-vision binoculars.

He focused in on the area directly in front of the terminal. Nothing of interest.

Reznick waited, and waited.

What if the guy didn't turn up? What if it was a ruse? How could he know he had the right guy?

Reznick was a stickler for detail. From doing wetwork, he knew the importance of being sure who the target was. He wondered if he shouldn't try and get in closer.

He liked certainty. It was ingrained in him. It was certainty that would keep him alive. The more he thought about this setup, the less he liked it. He wondered again if he shouldn't just get up close and deal with it. But the bottom line was there were no good, clean solutions.

He peered through the binoculars again.

Slowly, a man wearing a Seahawks hat emerged from the terminal into the periphery of his vision. The man stopped and stood in front of the terminal building.

Reznick stared through the binoculars and studied the man, who didn't have any cases or bags of any sort. Reznick could tell he was making an effort to stare straight ahead. Then the man touched his left ear.

Reznick zoomed in on the man's head.

The guy was wearing an earpiece.

Reznick scanned the front of the terminal building. A laughing mom with her two young kids, a couple holding hands . . . various people entering and exiting. He checked each of them over.

Then he trained the binoculars back on the man with the Seahawks hat. Eyes staring straight ahead. The man touched his ear again.

Reznick scanned a wider area, examining those within a twenty-meter radius of the front of the main terminal.

It was then his attention was drawn to a figure sitting on a bench by the taxi pickup, reading a newspaper. He watched as the figure turned the page of the paper and then touched his right ear.

Reznick zoomed in. His heart hiked up a notch.

The man was also wearing an earpiece.

Fifty-Four

Meyerstein was sitting in the back of the SUV as the FBI driver sped toward Bob Hope Airport. Three cars ahead was a plain-clothes FBI SWAT team riding in a Lincoln.

"Martha, the intercept has been analyzed, and from the GPS we're certain the call is genuine," Veitch's voice on the radio.

"What else?"

"We're using the airport's surveillance cameras. Looking at the guy in real time, cool as you like with his Seahawks hat on."

"Face recognition?"

"Nothing so far."

Meyerstein said nothing.

"I know, it's frustrating. But the hat, the angle of the camera . . . it's not allowing for a full-face scan."

"Who've we got on the ground?"

"Airport cops are aware of the situation."

"Listen to me, they need to back off on this. Likely this guy is going to have to be taken down."

"They're under strict orders."

"How many people in the area?"

"Thirteen people, in addition to the Seahawks guy."

"If there's any heat this Quds guy will take down as many innocents as he can."

"I know."

Meyerstein checked her iPad, which showed the video coming through from the airport. "OK, I'm looking at what you're seeing. Yeah, I see your problem. Face partially concealed."

"Martha, what's your ETA?"

Meyerstein tapped the driver on the shoulder. "How long?"

"Two minutes—maybe three."

Meyerstein said, "Did you hear that?"

"Copy that, Martha."

Meyerstein went quiet for a few moments as they sped through the dark Burbank streets.

Stamper sighed. "Talk to me, Martha, I know you too well. What else is bothering you?"

"Reznick."

"What about him?"

"He sent the text. And we've got to assume Reznick must be in the vicinity. So where the hell is he?"

"We both know Reznick will try and take this guy down by himself. It's what he does."

Meyerstein stared at the footage. "What I'm seeing . . . the profile is similar but I'm not sure." She watched as the man lit up a cigarette.

The driver turned and said, "ETA ninety seconds."

Meyerstein shook her head. "Roy, where the hell is Reznick?"

"My guess, he's there already. Watching and waiting."

That was exactly what she feared.

Fifty-Five

Reznick stared through the binoculars at the guy in the Seahawks hat smoking his cigarette. He was beginning to doubt whether he could take the guy down. His line of sight kept getting interrupted.

"Who are you?" he said through gritted teeth.

Reznick turned his focus onto the guy reading the paper, who was now wearing a Lakers hat. His hand was on his mouth as if he were thinking, but it could also be good cover for communicating. He was sure they were part of the same crew.

His problem was how to deal with both of them. If he took out one, the other would potentially get away in the ensuing chaos and panic.

Slow is smooth, smooth is fast.

Both needed to be neutralized.

He considered taking out the guy on the bench, up close. Then focusing on the Seahawks guy.

He needed to decide, and make his move.

Suddenly, the Seahawks guy turned his head. Two SUVs had pulled up in front of the terminal, blocking Reznick's view. He stared through the binoculars.

The doors of the first SUV burst open, and four plain-clothes officers ran out toward the Seahawks guy. The half a dozen or so people nearby dived for cover. In less than thirty seconds, the four-man team had the guy cuffed and in the back of their SUV. Then they sped out of sight.

Reznick's heart was racing as he turned his attention to the guy on the bench.

Just at that moment, Reznick saw Meyerstein emerge from the second SUV, cell phone pressed to her ear. He figured they had intercepted the message he sent from Morlach's phone. He watched as she directed operations while talking on the phone.

Reznick turned the binoculars to the Lakers guy and saw him disappear into the crowd like a ghost.

Fifty-Six

Meyerstein stood outside the terminal with three other Feds, and surveyed the parking garage opposite, phone pressed to her ear.

"Give me the latest on Sazegara," she said.

Veitch sighed. "Martha, that's why I'm calling. It's not him."

"What?"

"It's definitely not Mohsen Sazegara. It's his younger brother, Behzad."

Meyerstein closed her eyes. "Gimme a break, will you?"

"Martha, we're one step behind, all the goddamn way."

"The guy in our custody—"

"Behzad Sazegara."

"Why wasn't he on our radar before now?"

"He was a sleeper, Martha."

"If we had his brother under surveillance until recently, why not him?"

Veitch sighed. "Someone has fucked up on this, that's for sure."

"Well, that's just great." Meyerstein thought for a moment. "This Behzad . . . he was wearing an earpiece. What distance would it operate at?"

"Two hundred yards if it was bought from the Internet. Military-grade would be up to maybe half a mile."

"What about the travel documents that he was carrying?"

"We're looking them over, Martha. False IDs all the way."

"Mohsen's here at the airport, I know it. We need to shut this down."

"We're on it, Martha."

"Listen to me. We need to find him before this night is done."

"Martha, I said we're on it."

"We need to find him. Before Reznick gets his hands on him."

Fifty-Seven

Reznick had watched from afar as the other guy had slipped away from the crowd at the front of the terminal and jumped on a shuttle bus. He quickly packed everything away into the rifle bag and put it under the back seat of the BMW.

He got into the driver's seat and sped out of the garage. As he headed down a near-empty road, he spotted the bus.

Reznick tailed the vehicle a few hundred yards to the Ramada Inn. The van stopped at the entrance. The Lakers guy got out with two other passengers and went inside.

Reznick parked the BMW in the parking lot of the small hotel so he had clear line of sight to the entrance. He reached behind him to retrieve the rifle bag, and checked the rifle and 9mm were locked and loaded. Time seemed to slow as he waited. The guy might be holed up in there for hours.

But, less than fifteen minutes later, Reznick was in luck.

The Lakers guy emerged from the hotel, accompanied by a woman. He had changed his clothes, and a brown leather bag was slung over his shoulder. His gaze seemed to scan the parking lot.

Reznick slid down low in his seat as they crossed the parking lot to a Cadillac Escalade with tinted windows. The woman got into the driver's seat, while the man threw the leather bag onto the back seat and slid into the front passenger seat.

The Escalade's lights came on and it pulled away.

Reznick waited a few moments before he pulled out and joined the heavy traffic on the busy freeway. It wasn't long before they were on I-5 headed for San Diego.

He wondered about their final destination. Were they planning to escape across the border, nearly two hundred miles away? The woman would be the cover. It was a perfect fallback plan.

The headlights swept the freeway stretching out in front of him. The Escalade was cruising in the fast lane. Reznick stayed in the middle lane, out of the rearview line of sight, as he contemplated their end game.

Fifty-Eight

Meyerstein was buckled up in the back of the SUV, iPad on her lap, ready to head back to the FBI's LA field office, when her phone began to ring. She picked it up the same moment a message from Veitch dropped in her inbox. "This better be good news," she said.

"Check my message," said Veitch.

Meyerstein double-clicked on the email. A pixelated color photo showed a man with a baseball cap sitting on a bench outside the terminal where they were parked.

"Who the hell is this?"

"We've had to bump up the image size by three hundred percent."

"And?"

"This is Mohsen Sazegara. Airport security was focusing on the Seahawks guy. But when we ran the surveillance footage, we saw this guy on the periphery."

Meyerstein stared at the image. "Son of a bitch. So where the hell is Mohsen now?"

The sound of another new message in her inbox.

"We're checking a whole bunch of footage within a two-mile radius with face recognition," said Veitch. "It's caught this still image from a camera at the Ramada in Burbank, real close to the airport."

Meyerstein opened the video, which showed Mohsen leaving the hotel with a woman. "Who's the woman?"

"This is where it gets interesting. She's Rosario Lopez, youngest daughter of a lieutenant in the Tijuana Cartel, the least powerful of the big three in Mexico. The question is, what's a drug cartel doing teaming up with Iranian Special Forces?"

"Technological know-how, anti-jamming telecommunications—intel that's very useful for drug cartels. You rub my back, I'll rub yours. Probably getting financial backing from Tehran, and in return the cartel help Quds operatives cross the border to America."

Meyerstein tapped the driver on the shoulder. "Freeway, south!"

"Got it, ma'am." The driver sped off at breakneck speed.

Meyerstein said to Veitch, "Helicopter support on this?"

"Choppers are in the air. FBI and LAPD. California Highway Patrol are also in the loop on this."

"So what's their location just now?"

"We don't know. We've just received the Ramada footage and are going over it. I'll get back to you as soon as I have something."

Meyerstein knew that the smart escape plan would be to cross over into Mexico, presumably with fake passports. Her mind was racing, and she was running on empty.

As was her team. She was driving them to the limit, most of her team surviving on only a couple of hours sleep a night. She could hear the strain in Stamper's voice. But she knew that now was not the time to take the foot off the gas. They were closing in. She sensed it.

The sound of her phone ringing interrupted her thoughts.

"Talk to me, Veitch," she said.

"Fourteen minutes ago, Mohsen and the Mexican woman got into an Escalade. They drove away. Due south."

The SUV went over a pothole and shook Meyerstein in her seat. "I don't believe how this is playing out."

"It doesn't end there."

"Reznick?"

"You got it. CCTV picked him up in a BMW following Mohsen onto I-5, heading south."

"I want all our resources on this. Find Mohsen—and find Reznick."

"We'll find them. It's just a matter of time."

"We're clean out of time, Veitch."

Fifty-Nine

Reznick headed off I-5 and drove through downtown San Diego. The car he was following was more than one hundred yards in front. He switched lanes and followed at what he thought was a discreet distance.

He lost sight of the vehicle.

"Goddamn!" Reznick said. He punched the dashboard and drove on, annoyed with himself. "Gimme a break!"

Then, up ahead, he spotted the Escalade in front of a truck, signaling left. He hit the gas until he was within seventy yards of the vehicle. Reznick knew he was taking a chance getting so close. But time was fast running out, the border only a matter of miles away. It might even mean taking the guy out in the line of cars headed into Mexico.

The Escalade drove on for a mile or so to the parking lot of a suburban diner. Reznick drove past the diner for a hundred yards before doubling back and parking up. He was just in time to see the guy stroll into the diner. The woman stayed in the car, the lights off.

A short while later, the man emerged and signaled to the woman. She got out and followed him toward a BMW parked under some trees at the far end of the parking lot.

Nice countersurveillance move. Maybe another backup plan.

Reznick slid down low as the car sped past him. He waited a moment before following, still headed south. Before long, they passed the lights of National City. Deeper and deeper through southern California. Closer and closer to the border.

Up ahead, the BMW took the exit onto the 905 East.

Reznick picked up his phone and called Bobby Haines, all the while keeping his eyes on the road.

"Bobby, pick up for Chrissakes!"

Eventually, a voice came through the speaker. "Man, your tab's gonna be maxed out today."

"I'm heading east on the 905, south of San Diego. Very close to the border. I believe the guy I'm following is trying to get over to Mexico. What intel you got on this part of the world?"

There was the sound of keys being tapped. "Mmm . . . OK, can only be one place, man. Otay Mesa. Border crossing."

"But my guy is smart. He's a wanted man. Even if he's got fake papers, he's going to attract some heat."

"So what exactly are you looking for?"

"What do I need to know about Otay Mesa?"

"This area is within the reach of the Mexican drug cartels. They have money to throw around. It buys a lot of influence in and around the town."

"Still risky. Too risky."

"There's something else."

"What?"

Haines cleared his throat. "Are you there yet?"

"Just approaching it."

"If he has the right help, there is one sure way of avoiding the border crossings."

"And what's that?"

"The cartels have a network of secret tunnels running from Otay Mesa into Tijuana on the Mexican side."

Reznick realized immediately what he meant. "Goddamn. He's not going to go over the border is he? The fucker is going under."

Sixty

Meyerstein adjusted her headset as she sat in the front seat of the chopper headed south, the lights of San Diego below. She turned to the pilot. "Can't this thing go any faster?"

"Ma'am, we're going into a strong headwind. We're doing well cruising at one hundred and seven knots per hour."

"What's that in real money?"

"One hundred and twenty-three miles per hour, give or take."

"ETA?"

"Five, maybe six minutes, and we'll touch down at Otay Mesa."

Meyerstein nodded as the chopper dipped lower and headed due southeast. Her stomach fluttered. Buckled up in the back seats were three FBI colleagues, one of whom's eyes were closed, not enjoying the flight. She felt sorry for the guy. It reminded her of her father's fear of flying. He wasn't scared of anything else, but put him on a plane and he was stricken, clutching on to his wife's hand throughout the flight.

"Neil," she said to the agent, "we'll be down before you know it."

Special Agent Elbourne opened his eyes. "I'm fine, ma'am."

"Glad to hear it."

Her headset crackled into life. It was Veitch. "Martha, Reznick is in Otay Mesa, edge of downtown. Border Patrol has been alerted."

"Good. What else?"

The chopper hit some turbulence as they flew against the wind. Her stomach fluttered again. Elbourne's eyes closed tighter as the color drained from his face.

"NSA lost the end of the conversation between Reznick and this guy in Nebraska."

"Give me something!"

"Martha, our analysts have been pulling up everything we have on the Tijuana Cartel and their interests in Otay Mesa."

"Tell me something useful."

"They own numerous distribution companies in and around California."

"And?"

"They've opened one in Otay Mesa, but through a legitimate shell firm who launder some of their drug money."

Meyerstein's brain was racing. "So if the cartel owns this distribution company, it can only mean two things. They could smuggle Sazegara out on one of their lorries or trucks. But that would be too risky . . ."

"Indeed."

"Or there's the second option—out of sight. Something that takes long-term planning and serious money." She paused. "You wanna know how many high-tech tunnels go under from California to the Mexican side?"

"Son of a bitch," was all Veitch could say.

Sixty-One

The car's satnav showed Reznick that he was east of Otay Mesa Road at the intersection of Highway 125. He had tailed the BMW all the way to a nondescript industrial area of modern warehouses.

Reznick pulled over. He spotted a sign over the razor-wire-topped entrance that said *Ramirez Distribution*. He watched as the armed guard waved the car through. Cameras high up on poles covered the entrance from all directions.

This was it. This was definitely the drop-off.

He pulled out his binoculars and saw the guard light a cigarette as he leaned against a metal barrier, talking into a radio. He watched as the BMW crawled past a dozen or so sixteen-wheeler trucks and headed to the farthest redbrick building. The man he was tailing stepped out, followed closely by the woman. They punched a code into a keypad and disappeared inside.

Reznick scanned the rest of the compound and saw a gas-storage facility with tanks, and an adjacent pumping station. Self-sufficient.

He pulled out the rifle bag with the stolen guns and ammo, tucking the 9mm into the back of his waistband. Then he walked the fifty yards to the entrance and up to the guard.

Reznick pressed the Beretta to the guy's forehead and cocked his head in the direction of the gatehouse. "*Dentro!*"

The guard went inside as he was told.

Reznick looked at him. He had prison tattoos on his wrists and hands. Reznick pressed the gun to the man's head again. "Speak English?"

The guard nodded.

"Who were the two people who just entered?"

"Don't know, man."

"What is this place?"

"Distributions, man. Look, I don't know who you are. I just work when they need me."

"Who are *they*?"

"Mr. Ramirez and his family."

"Where is he?"

"I don't know, man."

"How did you get this gig?"

The guard said nothing.

"Tell me about that office block, the redbrick."

"What about it, man?"

"What's the code to get in there?"

"I don't know."

Reznick pulled back the gun's slide and the man scrunched up his eyes.

"Don't give me that bullshit. You know."

The guard said nothing.

"What the fuck is the code?"

"I swear to God, man, I don't know no code."

"On your knees."

The guard got on his knees and closed his eyes.

Reznick picked up the man's radio, clipped it to his shirt pocket, and headed toward the redbrick building. He moved to one side of the door and pulled out the rifle from his bag, quickly assembling it. Then he took aim at the nearest gas-storage tank and fired three rapid shots into it with the armor-piercing bullets. The sound of gunfire echoed across the concrete compound.

But nothing happened.

"Goddamn," Reznick said.

He took aim again and fired off three more shots into the tank before it exploded in a huge ball of fire. Reznick felt the heat and oil on his skin.

He stood back from the door. A few moments later, three heavyset Mexican guys stormed out.

Reznick immediately gunned all three down before they could take him. Then he stepped over their bodies and headed into the dimly lit, cavernous facility. At the far end, he saw plastic-wrapped bales of marijuana stacked floor to ceiling. He moved closer, catching a whiff of the unmistakable, pungent aroma of weed.

Reznick approached a black steel door. He tried the handle—locked. He blew off the handle with his 9mm and pushed open the door, which revealed a narrow vertical staircase.

Reznick put the handgun in his waistband, slung the rifle over his shoulder, and climbed down. The stairs stopped beside an archway door. He could smell water.

Reznick kicked in the door and saw that a tunnel lay ahead. His eyes adjusted to the low light. The tunnel was around five yards high, probably ninety yards underground. Wooden beams supported the tunnel's clay walls. Lights lined one side. He heard the low hum of what was probably a ventilation system.

It had to have taken years to construct. Millions of dollars in man hours and materials.

He crouched down, and started walking.

Sixty-Two

The helicopter circled high over the warehouse as flames licked the sky. Meyerstein looked down and saw SWAT teams fast-roping down into the compound from another chopper. Her headset buzzed.

"Martha," said Veitch, "drones on the Mexican side are showing a six-car entourage just leaving a cartel compound on the outskirts of Tijuana. Intel says they could be headed for a meat-processing plant, which is where the tunnel might lead."

"Do we know how long this tunnel could be?"

"Most are around a half-mile long."

"How long to get to the other side?"

"Ten, maybe fifteen minutes?"

"Goddamn." Meyerstein sighed. "What's the latest on Reznick's position?"

"We've just plugged into the compound's surveillance-camera system. He's inside the end building. Already taken out three guys."

Meyerstein stared down as the SWAT guys encircled the compound and fanned out toward the redbrick building. "We need to get Sazegara before he gets to the other side."

"Martha, I'm just being told we've got their radio frequency now. CCTV shows Reznick picked up a guard's radio and clipped it onto his shirt."

"That means we can contact him."

Meyerstein breathed deeply.

"I'm getting the frequency sent to the pilot now. Elbourne will get the field radios we keep on board the choppers set up for you ASAP, Martha."

"Good work, Veitch."

The chopper descended and Elbourne passed the radio to Meyerstein.

"Jon, pick up. This is Meyerstein, over."

She waited a few moments. No response. She was about to try again when she heard a voice.

"Reznick here!" he panted. "I'm in pursuit. Redbrick building. South side of the warehouse. Ninety, maybe a hundred yards down there's a tunnel."

"How far into the tunnel are you, Jon?"

"Couple hundred yards."

"Wait for backup, Jon."

"Forget it. I'm going after them."

Sixty-Three

Reznick kept his head low as he walked. His breathing was labored in the dank air. His heart was pounding. He knew he was closing in.

Up ahead, he thought he heard a faint sound. Hurried breathing, perhaps.

He stopped for a moment and peered farther down the tunnel. He held his breath and listened.

The sound was gone. Only the hum of the ventilation system.

He pressed on for another hundred yards. The tunnel began to zigzag.

Reznick spotted a figure just up ahead. *One* figure—a small woman. Just standing there.

As Reznick pulled out his 9mm, he heard the sound of footsteps and breathing. But from behind him.

"Reznick!" a man shouted. "Time to die."

Reznick turned and threw himself to the earthen tunnel floor, as the man pressed a switch on what looked like a cell phone.

Everything plunged into darkness.

Sixty-Four

Meyerstein strode through the compound surrounded by a phalanx of FBI officers sporting semiautomatic rifles. She approached the bloodied bodies of the three Mexicans. A SWAT team member was taking photographs.

Meyerstein turned to the lead SWAT, Special Agent Peter Rimmer. "Who are they?"

"Still to be identified. Cartel members, almost certainly."

Meyerstein walked around the bodies and into the redbrick building, accompanied by Rimmer.

Rimmer pointed to the far door. "It leads down to a tunnel."

"Why aren't we in there?"

"Steel door is blocking access. The lock's jammed."

"So how the hell did Reznick get in?"

"It might've locked automatically."

"Shit, we'll need to blow it then."

"Thought of that. But the tunnel could collapse."

Meyerstein shook her head. "Can we cut our way in?"

"That's what we're doing."

"How long?"

"Who knows?"

"I'm looking for an answer."

Rimmer sighed. "A few minutes."

"Get it open!"

"There's another problem," he said.

"What?"

"The power has just gone out."

"How did that happen?"

"It's been cut deliberately. That'll mean the ventilation's cut off—so no air—and the tunnel in complete darkness."

Meyerstein shook her head. "We need to get in there, now!"

Sixty-Five

Reznick was in pitch blackness. It wasn't long before sweat was beading his forehead and stinging his eyes. He rummaged blindly in the bag for the rifle as he lay on the ground.

The air was heavy and humid. The ventilation was no longer providing clean air. Finally, he felt the cold metal of the rifle barrel and pulled it from the bag.

Reznick switched on the night sights. He peered with his right eye pressed up tight to the optics. An eerie green glow.

Dust everywhere. In his nostrils. He began to taste it.

Reznick heard breathing, getting closer. He heard movement behind him, in the direction of Mexico. He turned and scanned the area ten yards or so ahead. Cement particles hung in the air.

He turned back to face the threat.

Out of the corner of the crosshairs, he saw a red dot on the wall ahead of him.

A flash of light. The muffled sound of a gunshot. Then a searing pain as the bullet tore into his lower back.

Reznick felt his mind slow down as he realized he had been shot. He swiveled around as the pain erupted in terrible waves, threatening to overwhelm him.

He pressed his right eye up against the rifle sight again. Through the green haze, he saw the woman, maybe sixty yards away, with a handgun trained on him.

Reznick clenched his teeth. He got her in his sights as she lined up her gun to fire again. Reznick aimed at her head. Squeezed the trigger twice. A double tap.

A flash of light. The smell of cordite.

The bullets tore through her head. The spray of brain matter was illuminated green in the night vision.

"Reznick! Jon Reznick!"

Reznick turned around and gritted his teeth against the pain. He looked through the sights. The Iranian was on him. Reznick was expecting a bullet to the head, but there was nothing.

He began to cough. He could hardly breathe. Tears streamed out of his eyes. Nose filling up.

Gas.

"Reznick! How does it feel?"

Reznick thought he was going to pass out. His heart was beating hard. Lungs burning. He couldn't move.

He felt his vision go.

Reznick feared he was going to die. With what felt like his last breath, he willed himself to move. He began to crawl through the gas, rifle sights tight to his burning eye. He crawled, yard by yard, back down the tunnel.

A figure emerged, gas mask on, handgun pointing at the ground.

Reznick was shaking. Sweating. He wondered if this was chlorine gas—a choking gas. He wanted to scream. He was burning from the inside. But he focused through his tears. And he pumped the full magazine into the figure in front of him.

Lights from the muzzle flash, the sound unbearable. The man collapsed, five yards or so from Reznick.

Reznick slumped to the ground as darkness engulfed him.

Sixty-Six

Meyerstein watched as the reinforced tungsten door was burned open by Rimmer's team. "Get in there quick!" she said.

With gas masks, night-vision goggles, and powerful flashlights, the SWAT team rushed in and searched inside the tunnel. Dust, dirt, and gas were everywhere.

The minutes seemed to drag, then . . .

"Ma'am!" Rimmer's voice shouted over the radio. "It's a mess in here."

"Where's Reznick? Where's Sazegara?"

"That's a negative."

"Find them!"

Meyerstein waited with the rest of the FBI team. She paced back and forth.

Seconds became minutes. And still nothing.

"Talk to me, Rimmer!"

No response.

"Rimmer, where the hell are you?"

"We got something!" It was Rimmer's voice on the radio.

"What is it?"

"I think it's him."

"Who, goddammit?"

A voice in the background shouted, "He's dead. No pulse."

Meyerstein felt like she was going out of her mind.

"Rimmer, identify who is dead, do you copy?"

A long silence before he spoke. "We've tried to resuscitate him. But he's dead, under a pile of rubble. We're bringing him out."

"Who's dead, Rimmer?"

Rimmer was coughing. "It's Sazegara. He's dead."

"What about Reznick?"

"Nothing so far."

A few minutes later, the bloody, dust-covered body of Mohsen Sazegara was dragged out. An FBI photographer stepped forward and took over a dozen photos of the dead man. "I want him formally ID'd by forensics, ASAP!" she said to the photographer.

"Ma'am, I'll send them right now."

"Do it."

Rimmer's voice on the radio. "Ma'am . . . there's a lot of rubble. I don't think . . ."

"Don't think. Find Reznick."

"Wait," he said. "I've got a visual on something. Bear with me . . . We're trying to get to . . . Ma'am, we're through."

"Tell me what's going on!"

Silence.

"Special Agent Rimmer, what the hell is going on? Will you please answer me?"

"It's the woman. Dead."

"Reznick?"

More silence.

"Where's Reznick?"

"We've found him."

"And?"

"Reznick isn't . . . Ma'am, Jon Reznick isn't breathing. No pulse."

Meyerstein turned her back on the other agents in order to compose herself.

"FBI medics?"

"They're working on him, ma'am," said Rimmer.

"Do not give up on him! You hear me?"

The other agents stared at her but said nothing.

The woman's corpse was brought out, photographed and laid beside Mohsen Sazegara. Meyerstein prayed Reznick's body wouldn't be next. Time seemed to have stopped.

She felt tears welling up. She dug her thumbnails into the palms of her hands to take her mind off Reznick. She thought of her father.

Never let them see you cry. You're a woman. Crying will confirm you're weak.

"They're working on him . . ."

Meyerstein was snapped out of her thoughts by Rimmer's voice on the radio.

"What?"

"They've given him a shot of adrenaline . . ."

Meyerstein heard a female medic's voice. "Come on, Jon, come on," the woman said. "Wake up! Do you hear me? We will not give up on you, do you hear me?"

Meyerstein pressed the radio tight to her mouth.

"Rimmer! What the hell is going on?"

"Ma'am, we have a faint pulse . . . We need to get him out of here."

It seemed like an age before Reznick was carried out on a gurney, covered in blood and dust, oxygen mask on, attached to a drip. She felt a wave of relief wash over her. She kneeled down beside him and clasped his hand.

"Jon, you're gonna make it, do you hear me?"

His eyes remained closed.

"You get him to hospital now, do you hear me? Chopper straight to San Diego!"

The team rushed to the waiting helicopter, and in less than five minutes, Reznick was strapped in and on his way.

Meyerstein rode with him, holding his hand as the paramedics worked furiously.

"Stay with me, Jon!" she said.

"We're losing him!" one of the paramedics shouted. "His blood pressure's dropping!"

Meyerstein squeezed Reznick's hand. "You will not die on me, Jon. Do you hear me?"

The hours that followed were like a blur. Reznick was rushed into the UC San Diego Medical Center as soon as the chopper landed. He was fighting for his life as the surgeons operated.

Finally, at dawn, a surgeon emerged from the operating theatre.

"Assistant Director Meyerstein?" he said.

Meyerstein got to her feet. "Doctor, how is he?"

"He's critical. But . . . he is alive."

"Alive is good. Thank God."

The doctor smiled but said nothing.

Meyerstein slumped back in her chair, relieved.

"We've operated on his gunshot wounds. Miraculously, they missed the spine and major organs. But he's lost a lot of blood. He'd gone into cardiac arrest, but I think the efforts of the FBI medics saved him."

Meyerstein nodded.

"He's conscious. He's very drowsy with the sedatives, but we think he's going to pull through."

"I need to see him."

"That's not possible right now."

"I said I need to see him."

"He needs to rest."

"I just want to see him."

The doctor eventually relented, and Meyerstein was handed a gown and escorted through to the ICU. She walked over to the bed by the window and pulled up a seat.

Reznick's eyes were shut.

Meyerstein felt tears spill down her face. "Jon, I'm so sorry."

Slowly, he began to open his eyes. Blue, his pupils like pinpricks. A smile, or maybe it was a smirk, crossed his face.

Meyerstein wiped her eyes. "Good to see you, Jon. And thank you."

He frowned. "For what?" he slurred through the tubes in his mouth.

"For being the most stubborn son of a bitch I've ever known."

Reznick smiled at her for what seemed like an eternity. "Did I get them?"

"You got them, Jon."

And with that, he closed his eyes and fell into a deep sleep.

Epilogue

Six long months later, the sun was setting over Rockland, throwing tangerine ripples across the water, as Meyerstein stepped out of her SUV. She saw Reznick at the far end of the breakwater, staring out at the ocean. His hands were thrust deep into his pockets.

She walked over the granite slabs toward him. He turned around and stared at her.

"Meyerstein?" He seemed genuinely surprised. "What brings you up to Maine? You're miles out of your comfort zone."

Meyerstein smiled. "Hello, Jon. When did you get out?"

"A few months back."

"You should've called."

Reznick said nothing.

"How are you feeling?"

"I'll live."

Meyerstein reached into her pocket and handed him a sealed white envelope with the presidential stamp on it.

"What's this?"

"Open it and find out."

Reznick stared at the envelope. "From the President, huh?"

Meyerstein shrugged.

Reznick whistled and ripped open the envelope. He pulled out the letter and read the handwritten note from the President.

"They want you to go to the White House," she said. "A special ceremony."

Reznick looked sad as he stared out over the water.

"What is it?"

He was silent.

"It's a personal invitation, Jon."

Reznick sighed. "I can't accept it."

Meyerstein hadn't seen this coming. "I'm sorry, I don't follow. Why not?"

"'Cause it's bullshit."

"Jon, this is an invitation from the President. He wants to thank you."

Reznick's gaze scanned the bay. "I don't need his thanks. I don't need anyone's thanks."

Meyerstein was taken aback by his response. "I thought you'd be pleased."

Reznick looked again at the letter. "They want to honor me? For what?"

"For your courage. For finding Sazegara. You did it. You took them down—the whole Iranian operation." Meyerstein moved closer. "I'm sorry. I didn't realize you would react like this, or I wouldn't have sprung this on you."

Reznick pointed over to an island in the distance. "My father used to take me out on his boat whenever he could in the summer." He paused. "Served his country, too. You know what he got for his trouble?"

Meyerstein shook her head.

"He got a lousy government pension and a shitty job in a sardine-packing factory. The bravest man I ever met. They didn't give *him* a thank you. Left him to sink into alcoholism and an early grave."

"Jon, can't you accept it for him?"

Reznick looked at her and bowed his head, letter crumpled in his fist. He dropped it in the water and it floated out into the bay. "I don't like politicians."

"Neither do I. But this is the President."

Silence.

"Well, no matter . . ." she said. "For what it's worth, I don't much like the President, either."

Reznick smiled. "He's an asshole."

"They're all assholes."

"You sound like my father."

Meyerstein turned and saw the Feds watching from the shore.

Reznick looked over toward them. "You got company."

"I've always got company," said Meyerstein. "Never a moment to myself."

"You drive all the way up here?"

"We flew."

Reznick nodded.

"How's Lauren?" she asked.

"Costing me a goddamn fortune. She got into some liberal arts college in Vermont."

"Bennington?"

"Yeah, Bennington. How d'you know?"

"I know a lot of stuff."

Reznick smiled.

"Well, that's fantastic news," said Meyerstein. "Thought she was lined up for Princeton."

"She was. Changed her mind."

"You must be really proud."

"She's a smart girl. Just like her mother."

Meyerstein smiled. "Can I ask you something?"

Reznick shrugged.

"I was looking back through the files a few days ago. And the timeline shows that it started with a call from Charles Burns. And then you headed down to Miami, and from there it all just snowballed."

"True."

"I don't know many people would've done that for someone who wasn't their flesh and blood."

"Meyerstein, that's where you're wrong. We were flesh and blood. He was like a brother. All of them were. They were all mean bastards in their own way, but we were a family. We fought together. And sometimes we spilled blood together. But we were always family. Always will be."

The sun had turned the water a pale red. "You're never going to leave here, are you?" she said.

Reznick didn't reply.

"I don't blame you. It's beautiful."

"It's changed a whole lot since I was a kid."

Meyerstein stared out over the water. "It's got something we seem to have lost along the way. I don't know what it is, but Rockland has it."

Reznick looked at her and smiled. "It gets harsh in the winter, mind you."

"So does Chicago."

He cocked his head. "You wanna walk?"

"You got anything in mind?"

"There's a great place . . . clam chowder and cold beers like you wouldn't believe."

Meyerstein smiled back at him. "That'd be nice."

Reznick stood in silence for a moment before they made their way back along the breakwater to the shore, the silhouettes of the Feds in the distance.

Acknowledgments

I would like to thank the numerous people who have helped with my research over the years. Special mention must go to Angela D. Bell, FBI, in Washington DC, who was my first port of call when I began the Jon Reznick series of books. She answered my questions with good grace and impeccable professionalism.

Many thanks also to my editor, Jane Snelgrove, and everyone at Thomas & Mercer for their enthusiasm, hard work, and belief in these books.

Last, but by no means least, my family and friends for their encouragement and support. None more so than my wife, Susan, who offered excellent advice as each draft developed.

About the Author

J. B. Turner is the author of the Jon Reznick trilogy of conspiracy action thrillers (*Hard Road*, *Hard Kill*, and *Hard Wired*), as well as the Deborah Jones political thrillers (*Miami Requiem* and *Dark Waters*). He loves music, from Beethoven to the Beatles, and watching good films, from *Manhattan* to *The Deer Hunter*. He has a keen interest in geopolitics. He lives in Scotland with his wife and two children.